C.R.E.A.M. 2

Yolanda Moore

Lock Down Publications and Ca$h Presents

C.R.E.A.M. 2

A Novel by *Yolanda Moore*

Yolanda Moore

Lock Down Publications
P.O. Box 944
Stockbridge, Ga 30281

Visit our website @
www.lockdownpublications.com

Copyright 2021 by Yolanda Moore
C.R.E.A.M. 2

Lock Down Publications
Like our page on Facebook: Lock Down Publications @

www.facebook.com/lockdownpublications.ldp

Cover design and layout by: **Dynasty Cover Me**
Book interior design by: **Shawn Walker**
Edited by: **Lashonda Johnson**

Stay Connected with Us!

Text **LOCKDOWN** to 22828 to stay up-to-date with new releases, sneak peaks, contests and more...
Thank you.

Submission Guideline.

Submit the first three chapters of your completed manuscript to ldpsubmissions@gmail.com, subject line: Your book's title. The manuscript must be in a .doc file and sent as an attachment. Document should be in Times New Roman, double spaced and in size 12 font. Also, provide your synopsis and full contact information. If sending multiple submissions, they must each be in a separate email.

Have a story but no way to send it electronically? You can still submit to LDP/Ca$h Presents. Send in the first three chapters, written or typed, of your completed manuscript to:

LDP: Submissions Dept
P.O. Box 944
Stockbridge, Ga 30281

DO NOT send original manuscript. Must be a duplicate.

Provide your synopsis and a cover letter containing your full contact information.

Thanks for considering LDP and Ca$h Presents.

Acknowledgments

I owe God all the glory for making this all happen for me by touching the hearts of the people who believed in me more than I did myself. He had greater things in store for me even when I couldn't see through my own storm.

Cash, you are a blessing to so many and don't even know it. Thanks for giving me a chance. Adrienne, I never thought I would ever know the real definition of a friend, but you've taught me every aspect of the word. Thanks for being my go-to guy. You have encouraged me in more ways than one, I love you.

Without even being said Katrina, Lakiva, Latoya, Markal, and Larry even with all the inconsistency in my life I'm very grateful for y'all. My in-laws, Antonio Woods, Kenneth Johnson, and Whitney, I love y'all as if you were my blood brothers and sisters. Thanks for loving what I love.

My children, Miracle and Knasir Moore, momma has done it again! Know that all of this shit is for you. Always remember that I am the sacrifice. I don't want y'all to have to see or go through the things that I have. I'll die a million times just for you to live once. Know that momma loves you!

Baby K.J, Fatman, Ty, Terrica, Nene, C.J, Shay Shay, Des, Dy, and Duck (R.I.P), remember T. Lunda loves y'all.

Johnny, Uncle D.J, Diddy, B.B, I love y'all. Aunts Angie, Sabrina, Shawarn, Dememtra, and Hope love y'all too.

Santanna Wagner, I love you friend and I just want to let you know I appreciate you. You and T.J are my family, and I wouldn't trade you guys for anything in the world.

Momo Cora, I know that I have done a lot of things that haven't made you proud of me, but I know your love has never wavered thanks for everything. Love you.

Jaikia, Jaicoby, Kayzon (R.I.P), Keaira, Aaleeyah, DeAndre, Lee, Diamond, Demong, Darius, Arnaesha, Arneisha, and Tony, love ya cousins!

To all my people on lock, keep y'all head up; Niketra, Shantel C., Deanna H., Demetricy M., Monchell H., Monique K., Tiara D., Tony boo, Kadisha J., and all the ones I didn't name.

Rozena, I love you. I can't wait until I walk outside of these gates and see your face.

Momma and daddy, I hope that I am making you proud! Keep smiling down on me and protecting me from the haters. R.I.P

Lastly, I would like to thank everyone that has supported me with my first novel C.R.E.A.M and if you are reading this that means you also bought part 2. Thanks for the support and the love. I hope that you enjoy it and stay tuned for part 3.

#C.R.E.A.M

Dedication

To all who've lost their lives to police brutality… May you
sleep in peace.

Discoloration
What do you expect?
My life I must protect
By any means necessary
My family, I won't neglect
Freedom is what I seek
At the end of your gun
Is how we meet
Shots fired, man down
POLICE BRUTALITY!!!
How is that freedom?
The only thing missing is chains
And whips
But you traded them in for the
Gun on yo hip
Quickly to pull with no hesitation
Cuz in your mind
He has a gun… no registration
But does that justify what you do?
Pull the trigger
Bang bang shoot
We only live to survive
It's all we know how to do
Selling CD's won't ever compare
To selling crack cocaine
So why harass me?
By any means necessary

Yolanda Moore

We only live to survive
Just making it
Taking it,
One day at a time
We learn to cope with the life that
We live
But the force of your bullet
Has left the world drowning in anger
And tears
So, what do we do?
Return in retaliation???
But it's only because of what we fear
To many Travon Martins and on
Your mind so many BLACKS to kill
As a parent how can we
Protect our children?
How can we stand our ground?
When there's a gun pointed
Point blank
For no apparent reason
I'm guessing time has changed
Back to slavery season???
It's time that we come together
For what God created us to be
Which is you and I
No us or them
No black or white
Or I'll never be one of them
So stop judging my complexion
Or the texture of my roots
That's the reason for my anger
And in your mind black will shoot

C.R.E.A.M. 2

I Can't Breathe!
~George Floyd

Yolanda Moore

Prologue
Cache
On Chill/Wale ft. Jeremih

Love is patient, love is kind. It does not envy, it does not boast, it is not proud. It does not dishonor others. It is not self-seeking. It is not easily angered. It keeps no records of wrong. Love does not delight in evil but rejoices with the truth. It always protects, always trusts, always hopes, always persevere. And LOVE never fails. Corinthians 1:13.

All this is true according to the Holy Bible, but in my world, all of this is a far cry from the non-righteous. Love for me has become a thing of the past and a lost memory. Well, I try not to remember anyway. However, when you meet someone that ignites your fire and makes you feel complete in a way that's hard to explain, it's not easy for those feelings to just fade with time. No matter how many men or women for that matter that you bed to try to fill that void, the glass will always remain half empty.

My world came crashing down on me long before I knew it. It all started from the one person I trusted with my life, who I called more than a friend. Most murders are caused when you are under the spell of love, then hate, greed, revenge, and jealousy, or all the above. No one could've ever prepared me for the things one woman could cause. Never knew one person could be that calculated. She'd taken everything left inside of my corrupted little life that was left. She shattered everything within me. She burned, clipped, and tied what I had left as if she'd gotten rid of the most important part of being a woman.

Aggression unopposed becomes a contagious disease is a quote that I've read over and over by Jimmy Carter each morning for the past five years. It has helped me tremendously. Today I will be released earlier than anyone expects because of my good behavior and good time from the classes I've taken. I was granted furlough, is what they call it. Yep, it's been five long years of my fifteen-year sentence. In the real world, five years happen in a snap of a finger and it leaves you looking around with a questionable expression but in here, on the other side of the world, five years leaves you left behind as if tomorrow may never come. If this place hasn't taught me anything else, it taught me how to be patient and humble. And let me not forget, to never let the next bitch see the side you don't want exposed because in here if you do, they don't mind taking your kindness for weakness. Over the years I learned that shit the hard way until I was finally able to process that in order to beat these hoes you had to join them but you also gotta be smarter. There is no turning the other cheek.

I thought about all the things and the people I left out on the streets. I kept hearing that nothing was the same out there, but I'll be the judge of that or at least believe it when I see it. What? There are a few more corner stores. New phones, cars, new slang? New hustlers on the corner? Maybe even a new style of dress, but one thing I know that'll never change is the heart of the streets. It was still grimy out there and you have to always expect the unexpected. As long as I kept that shit in mind, I would always stay on top of the game. This time around I am coming with a vengeance and no one will stop me anytime soon.

Chapter One

Cache
Find You Again - Kevin Gates

"Cache Price rack and pack. You're free to go," one of the C.O.'s shouted. There is nothing to take with me, not even my pictures. Nothing. For what?

"She'll be back," one of them dumb hoes sitting with a life sentence shouted. Instead of getting like me and trying to get the fuck out of this miserable ass place, the bitch was hating. Bum bitch! I had no one to tell me bye, see ya later or to leave my information to keep in touch. And I definitely wasn't leaving any empty promises to any of these bitches. Hoes are something else and it didn't take me to be a rocket scientist to figure that shit out either. I guess you live, and you learn. Either you fuck up again or you get it right the first time. They say a hard head makes a soft ass and I've fallen too many times to even count the shit on either of my hands.

I left all the prison shit I had accumulated over the years right where it belonged, in that cell. I walked to front control having already signed my walking papers and doing my fingerprints. The only thing that is due to me were my I.D, birth certificate, social security card, and all that other good shit they give you to be productive once you're free to go. But the only thing that mattered to me is that fat ass check of mine that I've hustled in prison for over the years.

I was being released to the O'Brien House on 446 N. 12th Street in Baton Rouge for up to six months or until they deemed me rehabilitated enough to re-enter fully into society. How fucking rehabilitated they want a bitch to be? What would it take? For me to dress like a Pentecostal in a long-ass navy blue or black plain skirt with a look on my face as if I have a thumb up my ass? I don't think so. Anything but that. For now, though, I'm playing their game by their rules. I wanna get this over with as quickly as possible though because a grown bitch with a babysitter is overrated. Really, on some PG-13 shit.

After receiving all that was due to me, I walked outside in the cool crisp air with my state brought gray sweatsuit and matching gray and white Nike running shoes. I must admit, already the sun on this side of the gate shined differently. The wind blew smoother and my chest felt light, so I was able to breathe easier. I don't have to worry about the manly looking ass C.O.'s hollerin' about count six times a day. Fuck eating chow like a bitch was in France. Fuck them greasy ass half clean wet ass food trays too. No more bitches watching me in the shower when I was opening the lips of my pussy to clean it properly because some of them hoes don't. They're afraid a bitch will smell fish. The dial soap definitely gets it out of them hoes. I could go on, but I'm not because it's never-ending with all the fuckery that goes on while a bitch is incarcerated.

As expected, my nigga Tony was in the parking lot with bells on to pick up his snack like he was there to pick up an order for Door Dash. He continued to desire me even after I confessed to setting him up and also robbing him. One was a dirty bitch and she'd played on everyone involved. The bitch knew it was curtains for that ass. For a while, she had me under a spell. Her head game was that official, but I had started falling in love with Tony even though we were supposed to rob him from the jump. Things of course didn't happen that way. The scandalous hoe let me take the fall for a murder I did not commit on another one of our jobs for a rich nigga named Thadius Graham. I didn't turn the hoe in or rat her out. I just put on my big girl panties and rode my sentence out like a cowgirl.

Maya, my ex-lover, had snatched away so much from me, killing the father of my son hadn't been enough. A'nett and my freedom had also been on her to-do list. Thank God I weathered the storm. The one thing she couldn't snatch was my mind. Yeah, I can admit I fucked up and let the hoe take away the one capability I owned and that was to make my life happily ever after. To be able to love. And even though I love Tony, I'm not in love. It would take the act of congress to change my outlook on love. The only one who would ever have my heart unconditionally was my son. My relationship with him still wasn't what it should be due to all this time I've missed out on. Bonding with him over the phone isn't enough.

When I finally made it to Tony and his car, he held out a dozen of flowers. He took me in his arms and kissed me like he hadn't kissed anyone the whole five years I'd been locked away. Once he finally released me from his grip, he opened the passenger's door so that I could hop inside. Closing my door, he eagerly jogged to the other side. Wasting no time, we got as far as possible away from the prison. And that's exactly when I knew all of it was really real. May 7th, 2020 had officially become a date I would always remember. It felt nice to finally be free from incarceration.

"Cache, did you hear me?" Tony asked as if he'd been talking to me for a while.

"I'm sorry, no bae. What did you say?"

"When do you have to be at the O'Brien House?" he asked, placing his hand on my thigh.

"No later than 7:00 p.m." My response was short. I was still busy taking in my surroundings. He had to understand, didn't he?

"A'ight. We've got a few hours to kill. What would you like to do? Hit the malls, eat? What about your hair and nails?" he asked as if any of that would be the first thing I wanted to get into after five years.

"I wanna fuck" I said straight no chaser.

"A'ight," he agreed, wanting it just as bad as I did. He U turned in the middle of the street not caring if cops were around. I didn't say anything, but I checked to see if we would be getting pulled over. I didn't see anyone, so I figured we were good. I needed to relax, but fuck I just got out seconds ago. I wasn't trying to go back any time soon.

On the ride, we hadn't done much talking and I was happy that we didn't. I don't know exactly what it is that I would say. "Where are we going?" I asked, not wanting to go to his house.

"Home. You cool with that?"

"Not really. Let's head to a room. Did you bring the things I asked for?" I asked referring to all the essential things a woman needed to feel like a woman especially on her first day home from prison.

"Yeah, I got what you asked for, but if you need anything else just let me know. I also have a few other surprises for you," he said squeezing my leg. He hadn't taken his hand from that one spot since he first placed it there.

Finally, pulling up to the hotel at the Casino Rouge, I felt a sense of relief. I was far from the prison and again freedom felt even more realistic than when we first drove off.

Our destination was room sixty-nine. What a coincidence? We wasted no time unpacking the things that I would need for the evening. The first thing I need before sex is a bathtub. I couldn't wait to lay back in a pool of hot water and soak my aching body and cleanse my pores. Living on the inside surely does damage to the body. The pillows were horrible as well as the flat mats we slept on.

Tony ran a hot bubble bath with lavender candles and bath beads for me. He also put a cap full of bleach and added rose petals from the door leading up to the tub. Gently lying on top of the bubbles in the tub also scattered inside were more roses. I must admit either Tony had really stepped his game up on his grown man or he knew he was definitely in for a treat.

As Tony took a seat on the top of the closed toilet seat, I crossed my arms across my stomach relieving myself of my shirt. Then my shoes, my sweats, and next came the white sports bra and the white granny panties. Nothing was sexy about them at all but still Tony looked at me with a twinkle in his eye as if I had been standing in front of him with the Victoria Secret's newest fall addition from the bra and panty section.

As I got inside the tub, the hot water made me tense up. It had been so long and not just for a tub, but hot water in general. That shit is hard to come by when you're locked up unless you get up before the six o'clock shift change. After that, it's over with.

Without saying a word, Tony dipped his hands in the water, soaping up a towel to bathe me. He took his time washing every bit of the five years off of me. My body felt cleansed, but my pussy was drenched and not because of the tub of water. In a sex, love, and pain type of way. That dirty shit that Tank spoke of.

Now on his knees on the side of the tub, Tony took his time washing my hair. He dipped me back under the now running water as if I was making a new commitment. I emerged from under the water as if I'd been baptized. I took a deep breath, but it wasn't because I was drowning. Tony flicked my clit with persistence and wouldn't let up. I could feel the nut building up in me, as my stomach muscle flexed each time, I had reached my peak this nigga would slow his pace and leave me hungry for more.

"Tony, fuck me. *Please*," I hissed tired of the antics. He had me wanting to fuck him and fuck him up at the same time. By the time we reached the bed, we had fucked and sucked each other so much the bed had started to look useless. Tony certainly didn't disappoint. Of course, we fucked on the bed anyway just because we could.

Lying on our sides in the bed, Tony had begun fucking me from the back. His right hand rubbing my clit. He knew exactly how that shit drove me crazy. His left hand gripped my breast. He kissed the crease of my neck sending a shiver down my spine. I needed to kiss him to feel even more deeply connected than we already were. Our tongues collided with one another as if we were born that way. He stroked the inside of my pussy walls each time he hit my g-spot flicking my clit and sucked my tongue all at the same time making my entire body tremble like an earthquake.

"God, how I missed this dick," was all I could get out before I started to cream all over his dick.

"I miss this pussy too. Fuck, bae. I'm about to cum." He growled in my ear like a lion. As he came, my pussy walls continued to pulsate, expanding, and contracting rhythmically encouraging him to get all of it out.

"Fuck," he cursed.

When the race to the finish line was over, we were both spent like we'd spent our last two dollars at a juke joint. Hands down he definitely had a point to prove. If he kept fucking me like this, I would proudly carry his last name. Cache Clark didn't sound bad at all.

Chapter Two

Cache
Life is Good - Future ft. Drake

The next morning, I woke up feeling the left side of the bed only to find it cold and empty. That's when I realized I made it to the O'Brien house, and I was no longer laid up on the side of Tony. "Damn!" I mentally cursed once I realized I wouldn't be receiving another session of hot and steamy sex with my man.

Yeah, my man. We'd work through all the bullshit that was caused by the actions of Maya also known as One, my ex. I regretted the day I met that hoe. If I only followed my first mind that day, we met years ago when I hit that sweet ass lick where we met. Things didn't quite work out as I planned. She became obsessed with me. She made me wonder if the shit she'd done had been her attention from the jump. I guess that's some shit I'll probably never get the answers to.

As I began to dress for the day, I checked my iPhone to see if I had any missed calls from my man. I didn't. What the fuck could he be doing to where I'm not his first priority? His ass could start tripping if he wanted. It was too damn early in the game to be fucking up. I wasn't gon' trip on the nigga just yet. I had shit I needed to get taken care of anyway.

First things first, I had to drop in by my P.O's office before I did anything else knowing they looked for any reason to haul a bitch back off in them silver bracelets. I grabbed my purse and made sure the car keys Tony gave me were inside. I walked to the front desk to sign out and get a bus card to play it off as if I would need it to get around. I wasn't supposed to have a car yet or a phone.

"Good morning, Ms. Cache. How did you sleep on your first night?" the administrative assistant of the O'Brien House asked me. *If you got fucked like I did last night, you'd know I slept in heaven,* I thought with a smile on my face.

"Krys Feltment, right?" I asked as if I knew her name but read her name tag without her noticing. She nodded her head just as cheerful as she was when she spoke to me. "I'm blessed this morning couldn't be better and I slept...peacefully." I paused searching for the right word. I smiled politely walking off since I was really not up for conversation this morning. I kept in my mind to play nice though. If these people didn't deem me as the rehabilitated person that I needed to be, I could kick rocks and kiss ass because I'd be doing the rest of my fifteen-year sentence. Fuck that shit. It just wasn't happening. I would hold court in the streets first.

Speaking of staying out of jail, I had to abide by all of the halfway house rules. I needed to obtain a job. I would work on that after checking in with my probation officer. I hoped my P.O. was a guy, but then again, I had a way with the ladies too so it really didn't matter. Well, at least that's what I thought until I stepped into the probation and parole office and my name was being called. This white bitch looked as mean and miserable as they come.

Still, I kept my game face on when I followed her to her small ass office. As she sat behind her desk, I took one of the two seats that are adjacent to her. I waited while she pretended to go over my file. She knew muthafuckin' well there wasn't much on the paper in front of her. I just sat there vexed as fuck, even though my persona showed I was as humble as a lamb.

"Well Ms. Price, my name is Amber Dicks." *Figures,* I thought and shook my head. "I hope you've learned your lesson because murder is a pretty hard offense. If it was up to me, you'd still be in the joint doing a life sentence," she said while looking up from my file closing it, and crossing her arms in front of her resting them on her desk.

Okay, I see I'm dealing with a bold bitch. I bet if that hoe didn't have that badge, she wouldn't have a voice, I thought as I continued to sit still not wanting to give either of us a reason to pop off. The only thing that would give me away and show how angry I was about what she said, would be the twitch in my top lip. *Keep it under control Cache,* I coached myself.

As hard as it was, I kept smiling politely regardless of my true feelings. I smiled like the white folks do when they walk past a nigga, clutching their purse with a tight-ass smile on their face.

"Do you have your payment for the month?"

"What? I just got out yesterday. I haven't even had the chance to look for a job. My first stop was you."

"I know when you got out. I just looked at your paperwork ma'am. And I don't need you telling me how to do my damn job," she said, taking her cuffs off her belt and placing them on her desk on top of my file. *Did this hoe just threaten me? Ain't this a bitch? Out of all the muthafuckin' probation officers, there are, I had to get a hoe with an attitude?* I didn't argue with her any further, I went in my Birkin and shitted on the hoe instead. I came out with five hundos. *Maybe that'll shut her ass up and keep her big ass off my back for a while.*

Handing the money over to her felt like I was being robbed without a weapon; straight up fucked with no grease! But money makes the world go around. If I wanted to keep my freedom, I had to chalk that up and keep it moving. Because I was definitely scared to go back to jail. Never thought flexing on a bitch with handcuffs would put fear in my heart.

"Good," she said smiling then licked her fingers to count two of the bills and place them in her pocket. Oh, this bitch likes money huh? Who doesn't? I should've known that. I knew exactly how to handle bitches like her. This appointment had just come to an end. I stood up.

"Where do you think you're going?" she asked standing up as well. I didn't even bother answering her. I dropped an extra bill on her desk.

"Go do something nice for yourself," I said before I walked out the door.

After leaving my probation officer, I really wanted to say fuck a job, but I kept the O'Brien House in mind. Later, I found a job and I needed to go straight to a salon. The first salon I drove by was the one I stopped at. I really didn't want to fuck with any of the bitches from my past and thought it good to start anew. I know I could've called my sister, Chanel, because she does hair, or she could've told me where the hot spots were. However, nobody besides Tony knew that I was home. I stopped contacting my family after that horrible shit happened to A'nett.

"Aye, yo Cache. What's up, lil momma? I knew that was yo fine ass." I heard someone shout before I could make it inside the salon. I looked toward where I heard the voice. I scrunched my face as if that would help me recognize the voice or the person it came from.

"Meechi?" I already knew the answer to the question. I just couldn't believe my eyes. We were from the same neighborhood; he was the all-around hustler. At least he used to be. I remember being a lil girl and the nigga used to try to fuck me. Damn shame.

"Yeah, don't act like you don't know who this is. Where has yo ass been? The hood had been saying you were locked up for murder, but you how the streets are. People tell lies before the truth and we all know a lie ain't shit for a nigga to tell, but I'd rather hear it from the horse's mouth," he said, falling all over himself. This nigga definitely wasn't the same Meechi I knew. I see what people talking about when they say shit wasn't the same.

I remember back in the day when Meechi was one of the biggest dope dealers around. He had the latest clothes, the latest hoes, and the best dope sold in town. The only reason I had never fucked around and robbed him was because I didn't like to shit where I slept. See, I wasn't as grimy as muthafuckas made me out to be. Fuck, I was just out here tryna get money just like everyone else. I still had a little self-respect at least for my stomping grounds. "Oh nigga, I know who you are. You just look a lil different that's all," I said avoiding his question about hearing the truth from the horse's mouth.

"Nah, not just different, baby girl. A nigga looks bad right now, but Ima shake back. One thing fa-show is if I don't do nothing else, I gotta keep it real with myself. That's the shit they tell us to do in NA. Admission is the first step. I'm an addict no matter how often I keep relapsing," he said as he lit a cigarette. He took a deep pull and held it then exhaled a cloud of smoke. How the hell his lungs held that much smoke is a mystery to me.

"Anywho, back to you. You sho' have grown up to be a beautiful young lady. I almost didn't know who you were if it wasn't for that gap between them sexy legs looking like you been riding a horse all day." What's up with this nigga and horses? Does he have a fetish? He had to be high right now as we speak.

"Look I'ma catch you later. I got important shit to do Meechi, but it was very nice seeing you." I pulled on the salon door finally but was stopped in my tracks. Meechi's boney ass fingers were wrapped around my arm when I looked down. I looked at this nigga like he'd lost his mind. I definitely wasn't a kid anymore. If only looks could kill.

"Look, I wasn't gone ask you, but do you think I can borrow a bill?" Damn what happened to crack heads asking for a dollar? "You know I always looked out for Ann." He smiled like that shit was supposed to make me feel better. This nigga really was doing bad. All his teeth were broken and brown. The last time I'd seen him, his grill was iced out.

Yeah, back in the day you might've been good for it, but then again if it was back in the day we wouldn't be here, I thought. I didn't give him a hundred, but I did bless the nigga with two twenties. That same faraway look he held in his eyes reminded me of my mother. That same shit was the cause of me handing him the money too. Plus, I even knew how it felt to crave for something. That shit is the fucking devil. On some real shit, I really felt bad for him. On the other hand, in this world, everybody had a part to play whether it was the good or bad guy.

"Make sure you get you something to eat too, man," I said before I finally stepped foot inside the salon.

"Welcome to Exclusive where only the most exclusive shit pops off," I was greeted by an aggressive-sounding woman. "I'm Klimax," she introduced herself, grabbing my shoulders and air-kissing me. She was definitely a he.

"Cache," I said back introducing myself as well. I looked around the place checking shit out. Klimax's shop is top of the line.

"Cache? Did you say your name is Cache, bitch?" Klimax asked, dramatically placing her hands on her hips.

"Yeah, why?" I asked defensively. Damn, I hope shit wasn't about to pop off because I didn't bring shit with me for protection. What? Should I slap a hoe with a stack? Damn. But then again, why would I? This is only my second day home.

"Bitch come right this way. Don't I have a surprise for you. The owner is gon' be surprised to see you also. Bitch, I know I'ma get a raise for this one, maybe even a paid vacay."

"The owner? I thought you were the owner."

"Bitch please, I'm only the shampoo girl," she said, dragging me and not giving me time to process what was happening. We went to the back of the building. There were two doors, and we took the one on the right. Instead of Klimax knocking, she burst through the door as if she owned the place. My heart dropped when we stepped through the door. I didn't know what to expect, but I guarantee I was ready for whatever. But to my surprise, kicked back with her Red Bottoms up on the desk and smoking a fat ass blunt like the boss she's always been was my sister Chanel. She was looking just like Ann back in the day.

Yolanda Moore

Chapter Three

Tony
I Don't Sleep - Lil Wayne ft Takeoff

Life is good. I woke up this morning with a lot on my mind, nothing bad, but I just couldn't believe my luck. My bitch is home from prison after five long years that seemed as if they would never get here. Seeing her walk out of them gates for the first time, I felt my heartstrings pulling in all different directions than when we were together before she got locked up. It seemed like my life is falling right where it needs to be. Cache was just the added cherry on top. I was getting more money than I ever could have imagined and soon, I would be able to meet my connect, the man that had made this all possible. Emilio Hidalgo. I have been dealing with his daughter Margaret on a business level and also for the past five years on a physical level. I can't lie, she been making the shit happen for a nigga with no effort. I know it had a lot to do with the fact that I had been popping that dick off. Fuck a man gotta do what a man gotta do. That rule just didn't stop with these hoes. When we first met, I knew off top I was fucking from the way she eyed a nigga. But now that shit is sweet, I was back thinking with my big head instead of the one in my pants. Her pops requested to see me. He wanted to put a face with the man that's been moving his coke like God moved mountains.

At the end of the week, I planned to make my way across the border to not only meet Emilio for the first time, but to also break things off with his daughter. Cold world. I knew I had to be easy with Margeret and let her down easy. Hopefully, we could both agree to disagree and keep moving on with our business relationship as only business. I never gave her false hope even though I knew at the beginning she expected more. We were both grown and even exchange ain't a robbery. As much as she wanted to break me off with that coke without me paying a dollar, I refused. I never had a nigga, or a bitch give me shit for free unless it was problems or pussy and I wasn't about to start now. That shit is against a nigga religion. I love the hustle turning ten racks into a hundred G's was nothing.

Today I put all calls on hold. I had some other shit I needed to do for Cache. That girl was my life, and I can't wait to make her my wife. Things started off on a bad foot for us, but it couldn't be denied that she was and always would be my better half. She was my everything and soon I'ma prove that to her. But first I need to hit up CO to see what them numbers were looking like since today was collection day.

"Yo," CO said through my car speaker.

"Mane, what's good? What's poppin' my nigga?"

"Fuck you already know tryna make a dollar out of fifteen cents," he said letting me know he was en route. "You the man with the fucking plan," he laughed through the speaker. I hadn't told him about Cache being home yet and didn't know when or if I should. I know they still have bad blood between them. He shot my girl and that caused her to lose our unborn child. She went with her move first by slicing him in the face first, but I already know it was because she was caught off guard. None of the shit made up the loss of me losing my seed, but I held the most regret. At the end of the day, I felt if it wasn't for me the shit wouldn't have happened.

"I wouldn't say all that, but you know a nigga tryna reach Bill Gates money. My nigga, the streets is big and hungry for what we've got to make the shit happen."

"I hear that shit, but look my nigga. I'm on my way to go smash this lil broad, Jenn, I met last night while I got the time."

"So, you gotta fit hoes into ya schedule, huh?" asked Tony. CO's ass was crazy.

"Fucking right, my nigga. M.O.B. Money over bitches til' we die, my nigga." See that's where we didn't agree anymore. I used to say fuck a hoe until I met Cache. Not everyone is bound to ever come across that special someone. I'm just the nigga that just so happened to have met the girl of my dreams.

"You say that shit now, but this girl Jenn might be the one," I laughed knowing that nigga had no hope when it came to love. He would rather be a player for life.

"Fuck all that shit. The bitch is bad, but she let me smash too fast bro. One thing you should also know about me is settling down with a bitch is for the birds. It's too many hoes out here for me to be with only one. Anyway, look though. On some real shit, let's link up later tonight. We got some important shit to do."

"What is it?" I asked, tryna get a clue what he was referring to.

"Look homie, you know if I could say, you would already know what the business is. We gone fuck with it later though. Now let me go holla at this girl so she can swallow my seeds." That nigga crazy.

"A'ight cool. Do yo thug thang," I said hanging up continuing in the direction I was originally headed. I wanted to get this done before it was time to meet up with CO. I didn't know what he wanted to show me, but I know it better be something worth my while. One thing CO knew about me was I didn't like wasting my time on bullshit because time was money and if I wasn't getting money, I better be getting pussy.

The stop I needed to make was by my jeweler. I wanted to pick out a ring for Cache. I needed to prove to her how serious I was about our relationship moving in the right direction.

"Hey, Tony, my boy. Where have you been? Thought you stopped fucking with Jimmy the Jeweler." Jimmy said as we both laughed slapping hands with a half hug.

"My nigga, never that. You know how it is when you in them streets knee-deep." I pulled back from our embrace. "So, what can I do for you? I got all kinda new shit in this muthafucka that I designed. The shit hasn't even hit the streets. Some one-of-a-kind shit. Chains, earrings, bracelets, even pinky rings. You name it, and if I don't have it…"

"You can go get it. Nigga, I know," I said finishing his sentence for him. "Look though it's not that type of hype. I'm here on some official shit."

"Word, my nigga?" he looked at me pulling his shades letting them rest on the bridge of his nose. "Official huh?"

"Yeah, my girl, she just got home from doing a bid and I wanna show her that word is bond and I'm really fucking with her. I wanna make her my wife. She the only one fit for the position."

"Marriage? She did a bid my nigga?"

I nodded my head. "Yeah, my baby is a lil gangsta."

"Damn dog." He must've felt Cache's pain. "Being locked up fucks with anyone that has been there and done that. I got the right shit to do the job. When you give her this muthafucka she'll be pregnant that following week. Diamonds like this make bitches wanna fuck. Follow me." Before we went to the back of the store, he locked the door so no one could come in. I already knew what time it was. He only locked the door when he pulled out his exclusive shit. He also locked up when the other shit came out too, like the drugs, guns, counterfeit machine, or when he needed to make fake passports and I.D.s. You could walk in this bitch being one person and leave out becoming a whole other muthafucka. Man becoming a woman or vice versa. Whenever I dropped by, I only liked to stick and move. Getting caught up in this bitch would be a straight-up cold blood sentence to life in the FEDs.

"My nigga, this is some hot shit," I said looking at the stunning pieces. I didn't have to look any further once my eyes landed on this one ring, I knew she'd love. The ring has Cache's name written all over it. "Give me that one," I pointed out. "That bitch right there gone hit you for a grip. I got some other shit too if you want to see it." I looked at this fool like he had grown two more heads. "Don't insult me," I said. This nigga knew the type of bands I'm working with.

"Dogg, you know insults are the last thing I'm throwing your way. I'm just amazed at how much money you spending on a broad. As long as I've known you, not even yo momma can get this kinda cake outta you. That's all. I ain't gone ever question my money though nigga, so let me bag this shit and get you a glass of champagne before you bounce."

"Hold the bubbly and the bag." Once he charged my store account, I was ready to go. Like I said, I didn't like spending too much time here. "Oh, by the way, she isn't just a random broad. That's my soon-to-be wife and her name is Cache." With that said, I was out the door just as fast as I'd come. I knew Jimmy didn't mean any harm, so I didn't charge the shit to his heart. I know if I'm surprised by my own actions the next nigga would be just as well. I can honestly say besides Cache, I had never been in a serious relationship. Cache and I were as serious as I've ever been with any woman. It was like cupid showed up. As Jimmy said, not even my own momma held my heart but that's a story for another day.

Speaking of stories, I had been a product of the streets ever since I could remember. Most might say the streets don't owe them anything, but to me, them bitches owed me everything and I had planned on passing around the collection plate until I was where I needed to be. When I did reach my goal, I was moving Cache to the islands or wherever it was that her heart desired. That girl deserved the world despite everything she'd ever done wrong in her life. I looked at her and saw all of her good. I saw her heart and accepted her flaws. I also understand that hurt people hurt people.

All I wanted to do was make her happy. Which was the reason I made up my mind to go with my move tonight. I just hoped she felt the same way and didn't tell a nigga no. I know marriage doesn't change a person, but I am more serious now than I've ever been about anything in my life. I wanted to show her my actions would always prove why words meant absolutely nothing.

My phone rang, bringing me out my thoughts. I saw that it was Cache calling, so I answered.

"Hey, my baby," she spoke seductively through my car speakers. That shit like music to my ears and made my dick jump. Reminding me of how I had her screaming my name begging me to sex her.

"Hey. What's up my love?" I said smiling.

"Nothing, you tell me? I see I wasn't the first or last thing on your mind this morning. You couldn't even pick up the phone and call a bitch on her second day out just to wish me a good morning. What's up with that?"

"You checking me, ma?" I asked knowing how to get under her skin.

"Fucking right I am. You think you can just fuck me like that and not have no holla?" she said with a major attitude.

"I bet you got your hand on your hip rolling your neck and everything huh?" I laugh knowing I'm right.

"Whatever nigga. Just answer my question" she laughed to catching on to what I was doing.

"I'm sorry love. I just had a few errands to run."

"And it'll never happen again," she demanded from me.

"Nah," I said trying to pay attention to the road, but I was easily distracted thinking about the way she deepthroated me.

"Nah, what?"

"It'll never happen again ma."

"OK, that's more like it. I'm over here by Chanel's. I stumbled upon her shop. I didn't even know she had one."

"Word?"

"Yep."

"That's good. Tell her I'm proud of her."

"I will. What you got planned for the rest of the day?" Cache asked me.

"I gotta handle a little business with CO," I told her not knowing how it'll make her feel with the past history they shared.

"Alright. Well, I was just calling to see if we were going to do the nasty before 7:00. I guess I'll have to go play with this pussy in my room all by myself," she said teasing me knowing exactly what to say to make a nigga go weak in the knees.

"You really gone do me that?" I asked looking down at my lap watching my shit stand at attention.

"Nope, you're doing that to yourself. I guess we'll both be making ourselves cum together. Call me when you about to so I can catch it over the phone like I used to do when I was locked up." She laughed, hanging up before I had the chance to change my plans.

*****

Later that night, I was prepared to go check out whatever it is that CO wanted a nigga to see. I knew our usual meeting place and the time, so I didn't have to hit him up to let him know I was on the way. I pulled up to the compound and on the outside, it looked like an abandoned apartment complex. I did plan to fix it up one day making them low-income apartments, but for now, I had other things on my agenda that needed my immediate attention. Different sections of the compound were run differently. On one side, niggas sold drugs, and on the other side, which is where I was headed, anything goes. That's why I was unprepared for the thrashing that I saw when I entered one of the units.

"Nigga, what the fuck? You not gon' answer my fucking questions?" Corey yelled in a beaten bloody face I couldn't place. Not because his face was unfamiliar, but it was unrecognizable for the beating he was receiving. I just stood back not wanting to interrupt whatever it was Corey was trying to get out of his prisoner. CO waited for only a few seconds, giving the dude time to decide if he wanted to give up the answer to his question.

"Nigga, I guess you choosing the whore over your life? The pussy that good or the hoe just got fire head? Let me in on it my nigga because I haven't met a hoe yet that can suck and fuck me enough to die over." CO laughed, shaking his head as if he found something funny and he was the only one in the room that got the joke.

"This is how we gon' do this. Whenever I catch up with this hoe, I'ma make sure I fuck her then nut in her mouth because nigga I just got to see why the cat got your tongue. Plus, the bitch be having all kinda niggas going crazy." *Alright*, I thought. *Now I see why he wanted me here.*

For over five years, I have been looking for that snake ass bitch. It's like she's a ghost. Whenever we do cross each other's paths, that's one muthafucka that this world isn't big enough to keep me on earth with. I still felt salty with how she did my girl. Plus, the hoe tried throwing a cross between me and Cache. The shit she did really could have turned out bad. Even though I blamed myself for the loss of my unborn seed, One is the real puppet master behind the strings and that's the sole purpose she had to go.

Before CO could come from behind his back with his tool, I fired off three shots in our hostage's chest and one in his face just to make sure the nigga was dead. I don't know what the relation was between him and One, but whatever it may be the nigga was just murdered for being guilty by association.

"Who was he to her? Her man?" I asked CO even though it really didn't matter.

"That was that bitch's cousin on her dad's side. Nigga, why all the questions?"

"They were fucking?" I asked with a sour look on my face.

"Fuck if I know. I just said that shit, but I do plan on really fucking the hoe before I kill her. Thanks to you."

"Thanks to me?" I looked confused at CO's madness. I don't know what it is, but I felt this fucked up feeling inside my gut. I let the shit go for now. I mean I did just kill a nigga. No matter how many times you do, it always feels like the first.

"You the muthafucka that told me the bitch had some fire head," he said seriously.

Damn! I thought. *How can he still want to sex her after what she did to him that night at my party?*

"Right." I agreed. "You a crazy nigga. Keep me posted and get one of them lil niggas to clean that nigga up in there. It's getting late and I still got a couple of stops to make. I'll catch you later," I said before walking back in the direction of my car.

Yolanda Moore

Chapter Four

CO
Hood Figga - Gorilla Zoe

Clean up crew? Tony is trippin' and that's exactly why he hadn't found this hoe yet. If you wanted a muthafucka to come out of hiding, you give them a reason. Instead of me ordering the lil niggas to clean up, I did what needed to be done. The clash between me and that bitch was inevitable and I'm not talking about the hoe One. If you ask me, Tony was wasting his time chasing her. The real problem was his bitch. As for One, to me, she was just a piece on the chessboard that didn't mean shit. Cache was in my tunnel vision and I wasn't not giving up until we met up.

Tony thought I didn't know, but word on the street was Cache touched down. No matter how secretive he tried to be, he should know the streets know everything. I couldn't let my left hand know what the right was up to. Tony wasn't the same nigga I grew up with. We both used to be gangsta but I couldn't say the same for him. I felt the nigga was moving too sloppy and it was all because of his bitch. All the changes between us had my heart conflicted. We were like brothers and had come up together. Usually, I could pull his coat tail when it came to snakes slithering in the grass, but it was something about this bitch that had my nigga gone. Never in my life have I seen a bitch rob a nigga, set him up to get locked up, and then he falls in love. That's exactly why I couldn't let bygones be bygones, especially after that hoe cut me across my face. Her days were numbered. I have been a patient man waiting on his hoe to touch down. As for Tony being in love? That shit is too far-fetched. He might not see it now, but later, he would thank me. If it wasn't for me interfering, it would take Tony to get bit in order for him to realize that he shared his bed with a snake ass bitch. I really don't get niggas. Always hollerin' MOB, but then don't live by the code. Just like they say live by the gun, die by the gun and that hoe Cache will surely be the death of him.

The corpse that I left inside the building when I walked Tony out, would get shit popping in the right direction once the body is discovered. I made sure to leave his identification on him just so it wouldn't take long for the medical examiner to identify the body and contact the family.

After pulling the hood truck around in front of the building, I went back inside so that I could handle my business with this dead nigga.

"Fuck! Nigga, you heavy as fuck," I said to the corpse because there wasn't anyone else to talk to. "Either that or I'm out of shape," I said, making a mental note to hit the gym on a regular from now on. I pulled my iPhone out of the back pocket of my jeans to call one of them niggas from the trap to help me. I really didn't want to put any of them lil niggas in my business but right now I don't have much of a choice.

"Yo, CO whatcha need?" Malik asked me, shouting through the phone.

"Nigga, really? Saying my name all over the line and shit and questioning me. Just get the fuck back here to apartment D12." I yelled through the phone agitated at that stupid ass nigga. Fucking questioning me, fuck wrong with him? I hung up in his face.

Not even five minutes, Malik is coming through the door breathing hard.

"Fuck wrong with you?" I asked his dumb ass.

"Mane, I ran."

"Ran? For what? You know what, it doesn't even matter. Help me get this nigga in the back of the truck." Once we wrapped the body in the blue tarp and placed him in the truck, we headed to our destination.

It is around 3:00 in the morning when we finally make it across town where I need to be.

"Yo help me unwrap and remove this nigga from the back of the truck and into the driver seat." Malik really was a slow as nigga, made me wonder what the fuck I was thinking to call his fucking ass.

"Mane, how we gon' get home?"

"Bitch we got a whole muthafuckin' dead body in the middle of the hood and the only thing you can worry about is how we gon' get home? Are you serious?! Nigga, if you don't start thinking straight, our home gon' be on a dormitory full of other niggas and fighting a life sentence or death row. Do as I say, and that shit won't happen now help me remove this muthafucka," I said really disgusted. I hated when I had to school these wanna-be ass gangsta's. This nigga worried about a ride I thought shaking my head. Fuck boy.

When we finally got this heavy-ass dead weight ass nigga situated inside the truck, I was ready to bounce until I thought about the change of clothes, we kept inside the truck for shit like this.

"Take your clothes off," I told him while I went inside the toolbox to retrieve the sack of clothes.

"Damn nigga my clothes too?" he asked but also going with his move.

"You know what? Fuck all this shit."

"Boom. Boom. Boom! I hit that nigga in the chest twice and once in the center of his head just for good measure. Before he knew what hit him, he was dead. At least he didn't see the shit coming. I hurried, placing the gun that I killed Malik with on top of the nigga in the truck to make it seem like it was a robbery or a simple street beef and they both were casualties of the game. And to me? Just two more muthafuckas added under my belt to my body count, I thought as I began to walk off with a smirk plastered across my face proud of my handy work.

With all this work I put in today, I was tired as a bitch. I'm going straight to the crib so that I could smoke a fat ass blunt and bust this nut. Nothing made me hornier than killing somebody. Besides that, I planned to get myself some much-needed sleep. Tomorrow I had plans to pop a couple of x-pills, get out my body, and hit club Vibes up.

There isn't anything else I needed to do for me and Cache to cross paths. Honestly, I had let that shit go between us. I was hired by someone anonymously. At first, I wasn't going to take the job but when I was offered 100 g's no was no longer in my vocabulary. I don't know why she is worth a hundred racks to someone, but I definitely didn't give a fuck to question it. That wasn't part of my job to care only to erase.

Chapter Five

Cache
The Let Out - Jidenna ft Nana Kwabena

Friday morning finally came around and I'm rolling out the bed again to start my day but not to look for a job or a visit to the parole office. Today made two weeks since I been home, and I was approved to have my first weekend pass. Thanks to money because that shit talk and bullshit walk.

I'm so tired from staying up until three o'clock this morning with Tony like we're back in high school. Not that I made it that far in school. Life has thrown me in circumstances that wouldn't allow me the freedom to educate myself. That's why I took advantage of the programs while in prison. I couldn't hustle these niggas all my life. What I look like sixty years old pulling a gun and talking about give me what ya got? So, if I needed to fall back on anything, I had a few factual things up my sleeve.

I needed to get myself ready for the weekend, but in order to do so, I needed to stop dragging around. As soon as I washed my face and brushed my teeth, I went straight to the kitchen for a nice big cup of brewed coffee. It's still kinda early, so no movement is going on in the house besides me moving around. Everyone else was still asleep, which is fine with me. I welcomed the peace and quiet. Sometimes in the mornings when everyone is up and moving around, I felt like I was back at Momo C.W.'s house with a bunch of muthafuckas running around.

After fixing myself a big nice strong cup of coffee, I went back into my room to check my phone to see if anyone tried contacting me. I had one miss called and several text messages. I usually don't fuck with unknown numbers, but I haven't had time to store everybody's number in my phone yet. I hit the dial button to see who it was calling me after midnight like they ain't have no damn sense.

"Hey, you have reached," the recording announced. "Carnel hit me back if it's important. If not, fuck ya," my brother said through the phone sounding like a grown man.

I'ma just try that lil nigga later, I thought and checked my first text from Chanel.

Chanel: *Sis, tonight meet me at Club Vibes. Wear the sexiest shit you got... oh and you can invite that nigga, Tony, you were telling me bout. Love you!*

Me: *Be ready in a few minutes. We going shopping. My treat!*

I hit her back and then checked Tony's message.

Tony: *GM bae. Can't wait to see you later looking forward to our first weekend together.*

I smiled at Tony's message. I don't know what has gotten into him but I'm glad he has been very attentive, even though at times I can be a bitch.

Me: *Club vibes tonight. Chanel invited us, meet me there. Love you*

I ignored all the other messages. They were from cousins, aunts, and uncles. Knowing Chanel, she told them all that I am home and to meet us at club vibes. I'll see them when I see them right now, I needed to finish dressing. I really hated that I couldn't reach Carnel. I tried him again and the result was the same, voicemail. I'ma try his ass later, he probably just hadn't woken up yet. I know he didn't start his day until after one in the afternoon.

*****

"Bitch, you the only hoe I know can get straight out of jail and take a bitch shopping without even looking at the price tag," Chanel said as we walked around Saks.

"You must not know who my momma is." I looked at her sideways.

"Yeah, I know the hoe because that's my momma too and the apple don't fall too far from the tree." Back in the day, Ann was something even in her drugging days. I've seen and heard a lot of stories about her gangsta and a lot of the stories I heard weren't nothing nice. Straight disrespectful but that's my momma.

"Anyway. Bitch, at this party tonight, I need your ass to be on your best behavior."

"Bitch, please. Anything I do is always my best behavior, good or bad. Niggas prefer the bad though. Oh, and my momma is dead. I don't need no other grown hoe telling me how to act like a lady and shit because I'm grown too," she said seriously as she continued to look through the clothes.

"Yeah, you grown, and I hope you got grown money to pay for all this shit you racking up on," I said just as seriously.

"Girl don't get it twisted my pussy just as good as yours and to be honest probably better." She laughed. "But for now, I'ma let you handle this bill cuz a bitch paying for a muthafuckin' house. I would hate to be fucked up how we were as kids and jumping from house to house," she said getting a little emotional and if no one understood her pain I did. "Anyway, moving on to this party. I hope they got some fine ass niggas in that bitch because I plan on letting someone hit this good pussy tonight." she laughed at her own joke holding her hand in front of me as if she was waiting for me to high five her.

"Girl please. don't let it be none of Tony'S no good-ass friends," I said, really thinking of CO and what would happen if we crossed paths. I made a mental note to get myself a handgun. Don't get me wrong, a bitch is not trying to go to jail, but I ain't tryna die either. Fuck that shit!

"Why not? Because I heard through the street's that birds of a feather flock together. And if Tony is good enough for you, why I can't fuck none of his friends? I didn't say I wanna have one of the niggas' baby. Shit, if anything, I'm tryna swallow them. I can be like the lady you want me to be and just let them put the semen on my stomach. On some real shit though, a bitch just tryna get her back blew out. Nothing more or less. Besides, you know I love me a dead-beat ass nigga. Them the ones with the best dick."

"Girl, you know what? That's yo pussy, do what ya wanna," I said shaking my head at her wild self as we made our way to check out. I took notice of how the lady at the counter eyed us suspiciously as if we were too "black" to be buying anything out of the store. I kept my peace and hit the bitch where I know it hurts. I pulled out a few stacks stunting. Her face went from apprehensive to appreciative because if it wasn't for us, the bitch wouldn't be getting that fat ass commission. This bitch better be lucky I wanted these clothes. As I said, I wanted to keep the peace I didn't come here for no fuckery and I hope Chanel could keep her cool too but knowing her that shit would be impossible.

After spending ten racks with no effort, we were headed out the door, but before Chanel could step out, she had to make a damn scene. So much for keeping the peace.

"Bitch, I know yo white uppity ass not sticking your nose up at us. Do you think it's drug money just because we black?"

"Ma'am, I don't want any trouble," the lady responded. She was afraid Chanel's ghetto sass would pop off. A few of the customers had started pulling phones out recording the scene. I'm pretty sure this shit will go viral.

"Nah bitch, it's too late for all that. Fuck the tranquility. Let ya momma know I fucked ya daddy for ya college fund, bitch." I started dragging Chanel's ass out the door, hoping like hell she didn't hear the woman call her a "black bitch". If I wasn't trying to go back to jail, I would've let Chanel go and beat that bitch myself. Something her "parents" should have given her a long time ago, but then again like Chanel said maybe the apple didn't fall far from the tree.

"Black bitch? Oh, I'ma show you a black bitch" Chanel screamed and charged the woman like a bull slapping that bitch silly. I know because I felt dizzy from the blow. My sense kicked in when I heard the police siren in the distance.

"Girl, have you lost your damn mind?" I screamed on Chanel once we got in the car.

"No, bitch have you lost yours? You should've been hopping on that hoe head with me when the color black came out. I don't give a fuck if the bitch was about to say a black dress or even a black card. I don't play that disrespectful shit. Especially from no white bitches, fuck all that shit."

"Girl I feel what you are saying, but a bitch just got out yesterday," I said exaggerating, "but trust me when I say if that white bitch would've busted the wrong move shit was really gone be poppin' in that bitch. Fuck a jail cell when it comes to you" I said navigating my whip with persistence through the streets of B.R. My heart didn't slow down until I was back in the hood where they thought all black people look alike.

"I thought you turned on a bitch, you know being locked up could have changed you."

"Bitch don't nothing change about me, but my age and it gets finer with time baby girl. But on some other shit, where the fuck has Carnel been?" He called me last night and I missed his call. I tried calling him back, but I kept getting his voice mail. I didn't worry about leaving a message. I asked, pulling up in front of her crib. We got out and went inside carrying all our shopping bags.

"Bitch, to be honest, I barely talk to brother. The nigga dropped off a few stacks of money once a week. I put it up in the safe and he gone again."

"A few stacks?" I asked with my face balled up.

"Follow me," Chanel said as we walked in her basement. Without saying a word, she went to a wall safe, cracked it open and I had to stop my jaw from hitting the floor. It had to at least be a million dollars stacked in that bitch.

"Where the fuck he get this shit from?" I asked. "Damn brother been doing his shit huh?"

"Ever since you left it's been crazy, sis. Carnel started hustling when you left. Momo C.W started not remembering, A'nett died, and you went to prison. The shit just wasn't right. As kids it was easy relying on you for shoes and shit like that but once you grew up them lil checks you sent from prison every month couldn't pay the bills. Not saying that we don't appreciate what you've done but shit out here so demanding sis.

"Carnel what?" I asked

"He started selling drugs sis. He turned to the same shit that took momma. On his drop-off last week, he told me shit was sweet and he was getting out of the game, so you don't have to worry about him fucking with it now more. "Damn I thought. I never wanted them to follow in my footsteps using the streets to get ahead in life. Some way, somehow the shit always comes back and bites you in the ass.

I didn't say anything, I just turned around walked upstairs, and continued on my mission. "We have a party to get ready for, so I'll deal with this shit later."

I was too afraid to ask Chanel the next question that weighed heavy on my chest. Who was my brother pushing drugs for? For now, I'ma let it go and later start my own investigation but in my heart, I already knew the answer to my question. I am my brother's keeper and I refuse to see my brother be sucked into the pits of hell. The same hell that has taken so much away from us.

Yolanda Moore

Chapter Six

Tony
All The Way Up - Fat Joe ft. French Montana

Money-Power-Respect. I thought with a smirk plastered across my face as I entered club vibes. I had slipped the bouncer at the door a hundred-dollar bill to let me through the door with the small .22 handgun that I had tucked in the waist of my Moschino jeans with the safety off just in case. It wasn't heavy or intimidating at all but would keep a nigga off me if a threat presents itself. Friday nights are always live, and niggas don't take days off no matter the day of the week; holidays included.

Even though this is supposed to be a relaxed night for me and to celebrate my girl's freedom doesn't mean I am not supposed to watch my back. I wasn't letting my guard down. The haters always lurked behind the scenes. Even the ones that smiled in your face. With that shit said I'd rather be caught with a full clip than nothing at all.

As I walked towards the bar it seemed like everyone and their momma stopped to shake my hand to show love or give me a hug including the hoes. They also tried slipping me their number, but it wasn't happening. I politely turned them down. I wouldn't dare disrespect Cache like that. I know how bae like to get shit poppin' and I would hate to be on her bad side. She had already made me a victim of hers once. Instead, I kept it pushing.

When I made it to the bar, I ordered a drink leaned against the counter, and watched as my queen walked through the door making my dick jump. She came through wearing an all-black dress, which I'm sure was designer, that hugged every curve of her body. Her Red bottoms were black too and she walked with an air of confidence that said none of these off-brand hoes could touch her charisma and she was dipped in it. She was dripped in ice. I smiled because damn! She wore my money well. That's what I loved the most, her cockiness. She and Chanel came through making the club separate like oil does when mixed with water. My woman is the shit, and I wouldn't trade her for anything in the world. I know that I'm making the right decision by asking her to marry me. With all the shit we've been through I hope and prayed she accepted because with her I endured the good, bad, and the ugly.

As she made her way through the club to the dance floor, she never looked my way. She was attuned with herself, but I know she could feel my presence. Just when they started dancing together, I noticed CO stepping through the door shortly after Cache. What is he doing here? Did he know we would be here? He couldn't have plus he always came here. I just didn't think about the shit. Fuck! I kept looking from Cache to CO. So far neither of them noticed the other. I don't even know if I have a reason to trip but just in case I needed to stay alert of my surroundings. I know how hard it is for CO to let shit go. I'm just hoping he would let this shit slide but then again, his rules are, "every action deserves a reaction" and I would hate to be the one to prove his theory correct. For now, I'll play the background and see how shit plays out.

*****

CO

As soon as I stepped into Club Vibes the pink lady x-pill I took kicked in immediately. I don't know if it was the atmosphere or the music blasting through the speakers that made me roll harder but I was definitely on another level. This bitch is jumping, everybody came out tonight after being cooped up on lockdown for a few months. This fucking COVID was spreading like a wildfire in a jungle full of trees. Now we on our first stage of Louisiana opening back up and already our death and virus rate is shooting up more rapidly than before. And not a muthafucka insight is wearing a mask either. Damn. Niggas really know how to fuck shit up including me.

After me and my niggas grab a few bottles of Patron, we were jumping to the ceiling wishing any nigga would. That's just how I'm feeling tonight like I got a chip on my shoulder. Like I said, it's my pill. Them jiggas made me do it. Fuck it I had to blame it on something besides the alcohol.

Just when I was getting shit poppin' fucking with the hoes and gassing them up, I seen the bitch I'd been searching for right next to me at first, I didn't know who she was. The slammer had definitely put a lil weight on her. That dress was fitting perfectly like a glove and I wanted to put my hands on her in more ways than one. But if I had to be honest with myself, I needed to put my hands on that real cash in the worst way. One hundred g's isn't any to come by with just a snap of a finger, but it certainly would with just a stroke of a trigger.

I drew my gun inconspicuously and dug the pistol into Cache's back. I could feel her body tense up and I had to let her know this wasn't a game. "I know how you get down and you can't smooth-talk your way out of this. So, trust me when I say, you make the wrong move and it's over for you, bitch!" I said calmly and calculated like the killer I am. I didn't want to make a scene, but if shit turned ugly, I didn't mind turning this bitch to a bloody massacre. I doubt if anyone notices because they were so turned up. I could pistol whip this bitch right here and now if I wanted. I thought about it, debating if I should.

"You so hard-up, CO. I never thought a nigga could still hold animosity for five fucking years. You must really have a hard-on for me." This bitch had the nerve to turn around and whisper in my ear all seductive. My dick jumped, this bitch knows she is sexy but it ain't about that right now. I got a reputation on the line along with them one hundred g's, which is enough persuasion to leave this hoe stanking.

"Bitch, I'ma show you a hard-on. Now get the fuck moving," I said over the music pushing the hoe forward to let her know I am not to be fucked with. "And bitch, I'm not going to repeat myself. I'm only giving you a few seconds to make it to the fucking door. Bitch try me and I promise I'ma turn this fucking floor to a crime scene. Hurry up." I pushed her in the back with the gun once more. I knew I had her attention then. She put a little pep in her step. I know she was looking around for the chick she came with, but I waited until she walked off the dance floor and sent one of my goons to entertain her. He distracted her while I figured a way to get this bitch out of the club without any commotion.

"Damn nigga, I'm walking. I do have these heels on, and this dress keeps riding up," she said as if she was the one with the gun. I didn't give a fuck though as long as she did what the fuck I said.

"Ain't nobody tell your whorish ass to put that shit on. Dumb bitch."

"Do Tony know what the fuck you up to? I doubt he does, so I suggest you change them little peanut-ass thoughts of yours," she said as soon as we stepped outside.

"Bitch fuck you and that nig…" As soon as I was about to let this hoe have it, out of the blue I felt a sharp pain at the back of my head. "The fuck?" I turned around with my gun raised. I came face to face with Tony and the bitch that came here with Cache. The chick had her heel in her hand. Did this hoe hit me with her heel? If I didn't have bigger fish to fry, I would have sent her back to the earth.

"Don't do it my nigga," said Tony.

"I guess the charade is over with, huh?" I asked knowing that I had crossed the point of no return. This is something I knew I couldn't come back from. We both had let his hoe rule everything around us. I knew deep in my heart he couldn't forgive me for the loss of his unborn child.

"Really my nigga? You know how I feel about Cache," he asked me, and I could tell from the look in his eyes that our brotherhood was dead to him.

"My nigga this hoe made you change. You are no longer the muthafucka that I grew up with. I don't know you anymore!" I shouted back at Tony while we stood in the middle of the club vibes parking lot.

"Nigga, listen to what the fuck you saying! I grew up! I changed for the better, not for the worst. I love you like a brother. My blood and this some shit I would never do to you, no matter how much you change. Wanna know why? Because no matter what my love would never change. I'm so fucking disgusted with you. I can't even look at your face no more and respect the 'man' you've become." Tony said as he held his hand out for Cache to come. When she reached him, and they began to walk off I lost it.

"Nigga, so you really fucking with this hoe the long way, huh? Y'all in cahoots? Nigga, it's supposed to be bro's before hoes," I said as I raised my gun and started shooting. Everything from there moved in slow motion. Cache was hit first. Tony pushed her to the ground catching the rest. It was like I froze in time. I fucked up! Those shots were not meant for him. He hit the ground landing on top of Cache.

"Fuck!" I threw both of my hands up on my head. "What the fuck did I do?" I asked myself out loud. When I looked back up at the chick that was with Cache, she had been standing over Tony and Cache crying and screaming. Before I knew what she was doing she came up with a gun from behind Tony's back. In that moment, I had three options, kill, be killed, or get the fuck while I had the time. I knew the cops would be on their way soon and I would rather not deal with them.

Before the chick had a chance to think about what she was doing, I was out of sight but definitely not out of mind.

Chapter Seven

Cache
Devils - Lil Boosie

Breathe. Breathe, I encouraged myself as I ran for my life. My intuition told me that I needed to separate myself for what? I wasn't sure of, but I didn't want to take the chance of finding out either. In a full sprint, I couldn't slow down even if I wanted to. I could hear and feel the blood rushing in my body which was a sure sign of an adrenaline rush.

I needed out of this maze, but it's like breaking the DaVinci code. I kept looking behind me, but I didn't see anyone or anything approaching in a way that I should be alarmed. Only the darkness.

"Please! Help me!" I shouted knowing that my attempt to call for help had fallen on deaf ears.

Thump.

"Fuck!" I slipped and fell in a warm sticky liquid that felt thick as syrup. Swiping my hand on my white V-neck turned my tee-shirt into a murder scene. "What the fuck?" I said scrunching my face wondering where all the blood had come from. I looked toward the floor once more realizing I'm surrounded by my own blood. In a panic, I hastily searched my body for any indication of harm or foul play.

There wasn't anything as far as I could see but then for the first time, I felt a pain in my stomach like I was having a miscarriage. A fierce pain surged through my body that could have knocked me off my feet but that had already occurred. If I didn't know any better, I would have thought someone had gone inside of me and ripped my uterus out.

Someone in a black hoodie was standing over me. Trying my best to place the shadowed face, my mind came up empty. I did recognize those wicked eyes and that devious smile, but everything else was unfamiliar. I couldn't pinpoint my recognition. What I did know from the silhouette that I was dealing with a woman, but couldn't understand why she would want to bring harm to me or my child. Fuck, a child I didn't even know I was pregnant with.

Still standing over me at 5'6" and around 165 pounds, that didn't intimidate me. What did catch my attention though was her standing over me with what looked like the biggest knife she could find. That shit put fear in my heart only because I didn't want any harm done to the baby. This was my chance for killing Tony's first child when I had the abortion. Maybe this was payback because now I wanted this baby.

With her weapon raised above her head and wearing a villainous smile, I knew that I was in danger. My survival tactics kicked in and I braced myself for the karma I deserved for all the shit I did over the years. I grabbed my stomach as my mother instincts kicked in. I prayed that by the grace and forgiveness of God my unborn child would survive.

"Lord let me be the sacrifice and no harm shall come upon my child," I finished my prayer just as she struck.

Before I knew it, I emanated a brooding air realizing that my terror was only a horrible dream. Still seated on the couch at the hospital brought a little comfort but even still that didn't stop me from checking my body for any harm. I looked over at Tony and he was also safe and sound, at least as safe as he could be. After CO shot him in the parking lot of club vibes has put me on edge in my heart, I know those bullets were meant for me. I couldn't help but think how this could've been me it's really been fucking with my head. The doctors said that he had made it through the worst part. Thank God it had come and gone and the waiting game was over. He would be going home any day now. I guess that's where all the nightmares had come from because I dreaded my reality.

This shit had started to take a toll on me. What I didn't get though was me dreaming of a woman. That shit had to be because I hadn't taken one out. Like I said this earth isn't big enough for us three. CO had already signed his death certificate. I have just been so caught up here at the hospital I hadn't had time to get the ball rolling.

I stepped inside the small bathroom that is adjacent to where I sat. I splashed water on my face once I entered. I grabbed both sides of the sink balancing myself as I let the water drip from my face. I needed to take a moment to digest what had transpired that caused the corruption of my physical and mental state of me and Tony's being.

I thought I was out of the danger zone when Tony came to my rescue. That was until I heard gunshots then my arm being grazed by a bullet. The bullet burned almost sending me into shock until I realized it was only a gentle kiss compared to the bullets that smashed vigorously into Tony's back. I for sure thought it was over for him, but the script hadn't been written that way.

This had transpired over a month ago and he is still here to tell the story. From the doctor's prognosis, everything would be just fine. I could only hope so because what I saw that day told a different story. I only could rely on one thing and that was prayer. I wasn't looking forward to becoming another statistic, black, young, and a single mother on welfare while working part-time at a fast-food joint because the rest of my time would be dedicated to changing diapers and reporting to my appointments to keep up with food stamps and Section 8. I didn't want that for myself and certainly not for my child. My baby didn't ask to be here and didn't need to be brought into a world of uncertainty. A world that was surrounded by violence and negligence. And let's not forget this new man-made virus of COVID-19.

All this shit made me think of my son. I have been out of jail for over a month and I still haven't been by Knowledge's mom's house to see him yet. The one thing stopping me was myself. I didn't want to be to him what my mom had become to us, inconsistent. I was afraid I would somehow let him down again. That's why I'm so hell-bent on not going back to the slammer.

Deciding to go get some fresh air because these walls were closing in on me, I grabbed my designer shades before starting on my way. I could only imagine how I looked and didn't need the world seeing the stress etched across my face. I hoped Gucci did a good job hiding my pain. Fuck, I spent enough money on them bitches to do something.

I needed something to come full circle because even though I didn't want to become what the "world" viewed as the average black woman; I didn't want to give Tony up either. I knew he came with a big price. What's living when you can't be with the one you love? I'm ready to dead all beef. CO and One had to go. I refused to let them bitches breathe the same air as me. As long as they did, there just wouldn't be enough oxygen for the three of us. They had to go. There wasn't any negotiating, not this time. The good girl inside of me had checked out.

*****

"Cache Price?" Two men approached me from behind. Detectives. I could tell from their cheap shoes. Instantly, my mind went to an interrogation. I wasn't willing to answer any more of their questions.

"Detectives, I have already told you all that I know. Black man, black gun and I couldn't see his face, so I have no details for you," I said, realizing for the first time it wasn't the same two detectives who've been harassing me about the shooting.

"What, they sent some more of y'all thinking my narrative gone change because we share the same skin color?" I said laughing, knowing the games them muthafuckas played. Next, they gon' try to tell me a story about feeling sorry for me. Don't let the streets handle this beef, but let them arrest the person for placing my boyfriend up there in that hospital bed. All that extra bullshit. I just really wasn't in the mood to play this cat and mouse game.

"Ms. Price, we aren't here for that. We came to speak with you about Malik Johnson and Carnel Price." My heart damned near jumped out of my chest when I heard my brother's name.

What kind of trouble has he gotten himself into? Could whatever the detectives had to say have anything to do with the reason he hasn't answered his phone? With the shit that has transpired in my life lately, I haven't had the chance to check Tony on my suspicion. Did my brother sell drugs for him? That's when it tumbled down on me all at once. They didn't introduce themselves as narcotics, but instead as detectives. In that instant, I had begun to put the pieces together. My brother hadn't answered his phone because he couldn't.

The detectives were saying something about finding the bodies in a rural area.

"Right now, we can't determine if the case is a robbery gone bad. Your brother had been found in a truck with the guy Malik shot dead on the ground beside the truck." Maybe they had the wrong person I thought. "We only found a driver's license on both victims. We need you to come and identify his body as soon as possible." My head had started to become dizzy and that's when everything around me went black.

Yolanda Moore

Chapter Eight

Margaret
Medicine - Queen Naija

"I bet you start loving me soon as you see me with someone else, somebody better than you." You couldn't tell me shit I was singing, smiling, and in my glory. Why? Because I was headed to Baton Rouge, LA from across the Mexican border. This nigga Tony had me fucked up. What? Did he expect me to just lay flat while he played house with another bitch? I don't think so I'm coming for that ass with a vengeance. I'm just not that type of girl that he could easily persuade. I'm not gone lie for a while I had begun to lose my mind, but I knew exactly how to get this nigga under control, cut that ass off. And I am not talking about pussy I'm speaking of cocaine. OK let me stop stunting and at least be honest with my muthafuckin self. I know I'm not the first won't be the last to go through this same hood shit. This shit is even happening in the white house. Nothing but the scandal. If you don't believe it, think back to Monica Lewinsky and that blue dress.

Anyway, almost five years ago that sexy, chocolate ass nigga Antonio Clark started fucking me like it was his last time before he received the lethal injection on death row. I must say his young ass knew exactly how to rock my world. He rocked it so well that he knocked my ass up. The pussy wasn't the only thing he got a whole of. The dick is so superb that he knocked, or shall I say something more appropriate, he fucked the good sense that I had right out my head. That's just what a taste of good dick does to you unexpectedly. But as I've said all along, I need to sway him just a little and have him right back where I needed him.

The thing is I know I have a good, tight, wet, pussy but maybe I didn't contract my walls enough to grab his attention. I definitely didn't expect the nigga to leave me for some bum bitch from his past name Cache who in the fuck in their right mind names their child Cache? I have to own my flaws because I have been cyber stalking mami. Don't get me wrong, the hoe is beautiful. If I must say so myself. She's definitely a diamond in the rough. She couldn't touch a bitch like me though with a two feet pole or is it ten feet? My point is she can't fuck with me. I'm Tony's ride or die. You would think if he had a brain, he would be fucking with a real woman like me but instead, this wanna-be Atlanta housewife barbie bitch gets every part of him that I deserve. Yeah, I sucked and fucked and caught the nigga cum and swallowed enough to be the one who bags the ring. Niggas these days, I tell ya, would rather fuck with bitches that need to be put on instead of a woman that has already been crowned Queen. Muthafuckas loved to be needed and Tony's is just one of them niggas.

For the life of me, I couldn't understand how this bitch did it, but she did. I never thought another bitch would be a problem. I thought he was finished with her after all the shit she put him through but that's what I get for thinking. At first when we first started fucking a ring never crossed my mind. I thought why I needed any nigga to buy me a ring when I could afford one for each finger and toe if that's what my heart desired. That's what I thought until I realized I had competition like I was featured on *The Bachelor* trying to win the spot of becoming the bachelorette. Now I see the whole time he has been handling me like some project bitch. I could've gotten forty dollars and a happy meal. I mean I'm just calling it how I see it.

They had been posting shit all over the gram about their love life and shit like that. I've even seen that he'd been shot and survived. Life sucks! Tony failed to tell me he was once again fucking his ex-bitch. Damn! Especially how he was all in my DM telling me he was coming to Mexico to fuck with me, even though

I know he was only coming for business. That shit still wouldn't have stopped me from getting me a little dick on the side. I went straight *Kill Bill Volume One* on his ass hooked up with his best friend Mr. Corey Lane, but let me say this, never let a lil boy do a grown man job. His simple ass couldn't do the one thing I paid him to do. I thought one hundred grand was well worth getting the job done but I guess I gotta kill this bitch Cache myself.

*****

Once I made it to Baton Rouge, I drove straight to the hospital parked in the emergency entrance and went to his room. I didn't even collect the two hundred dollars when I passed go. I thought that message on the gram would've made his ass be a little more careful. *His ass isn't that bold to try me.* He knew I'm not dealing with a full deck and had hired guns to stand behind little ole me. I mean my father is Emilio. I didn't even give a fuck about my own sister, so I hope this bitch didn't think I gave a fuck about her. Rest in Peace sister, Rest in peace. Poor baby, she didn't even see it coming. As for her no-good boyfriend? I killed his ass too. He had to go. Why? Because if he thought he could fuck me and leave me, he had another thing coming. But that's another story for a different day.

When I made it to Tony's room, I was so relieved to see he was there by himself. Some bitch he got. I would've never left his side not even for a second. I'm glad she wasn't there in the room because I would've hated to cut up and my ass ends up at their parish jail. Me and a jail cell don't get along and green is not one of my favorite colors. However, though I came prepared, ready for war with my box cutter under my tongue and my body dipped in Vaseline just in case this ghetto bitch wanted to jump but things didn't happen like that. Cache needed to count her blessings because, for me, she wasn't in the right place at the wrong time.

I quickly cut Tony's air supply and got the fuck out of there. Talk about if I can't have him, neither can she type shit. Not to mention that my favorite show is *Fatal Attraction* on the ID Channel. I started to wonder if I had made a mistake, but quickly shook that thought out of my head. I didn't want my child to be fatherless but this the shit he asked for. Fuck it with the type of money I have I can buy a baby dad.

Right now, I had no plan on how I would get at CO or Cache, but they were at the top of my agenda. And please let me not forget Maya, she also had to go.

"Hello," I answered my phone once I was back in my car.

"What's up with the rest of my money?" CO said. I know he was calling to see where I was.

"Nothing. I'm crossing over as we speak," I said lying just in case I needed an alibi

"Shit yeah, that's what I'm talking bout." I know he thought he'd get the other half of his money, but it wasn't happening. He had me fucked up if he thought I was that stupid to not know he fucked up and didn't kill the bitch I put the hit out on. He definitely has earned a bullet for that one.

"Look, we going to link up later in the week," I said, hanging the phone up before he could say anything else. Whenever we got on the conversation of money, murder, or mayhem I would end the conversation before it could even get started. My father has avoided getting indicted and I planned to do the same thing. Dead muthafuckas can't talk.

Chapter Nine

Cache
FYM - Meek Mill ft Boosie Bad Azz

Too much shit was going on in my life. In the last forty-eight hours I had gotten the worst news of my life just when I thought nothing else could fail me. Somehow, Tony's air supply had been out the doctors said there was no way it could've happened unless someone touched it. The shit is really crazy because I have been by his side since day one. I only left for a second, but it had to have happened then. The detectives went to the security room ran the surveillance back and saw a woman coming and going. So, I was asked to come down to see if I could identify the person in the video.

The news also aired about my brother being murdered is the worst blow of the two. The two detectives told me it looks like he'd been robbed, and the stick-up kid left his pockets turned inside out. They hadn't determined if the dud malik robbed and or set him up, but he was left dead too. At first, I didn't get it but as soon as I started putting the pieces together, I instantly lost the strength in my legs and everything surrounding me went black. I guess I had collapsed in the right place because when I came back, I was surrounded by nurses and doctors within a snap of a finger.

After I pulled myself together, I hadn't even thought of calling my family because I had revenge on my mind and needed to get to the security room. Whoever it is on the footage could just as well be someone in cahoots with CO. I needed answers and I needed them now. When I stepped into the room, the detectives were waiting on me inside.

"I'm glad to see that you are alright Ms. Price. Come in and have a seat." I did. Instead of them flicking the computer monitor on and getting down to business, the detectives pulled up a chair on side of me as if we had ordered lunch and were about to break bread together.

"Ms. Price, we weren't properly introduced earlier at the hospital. I'm Detective Johnson and this is Detective Tate. We would first like to apologize for your loss and we're doing the best we can to find the person or people responsible. We do have few questions we would like to ask you before we move on to the unidentified person on the video screen coming and going out of Antonio Clark's hospital room. Are you ok with that?" Detective Johnson asked me.

"Yeah, that's fine," I said ready to get this over with as quickly as possible. I'm still in a trance from the news of my brother. I didn't know how I was going to tell Chanel, but I know it had to be done.

"Alright, where were you on the night of August 8th, 2020? At around midnight." That must be the night my brother had been killed.

"I was staying at the O'Brien House on 12th Street."

"The O'Brien House?" Detective Tate asked with a look of confusion on his face. It was as if I had just told him something that he'd rather me kept a secret. I know what the look was all about because 12th Street is known for drug dealers, addicts, and prostitutes. My appearance screamed money, but my attitude said southside baby, so I understood his confused look. However, you should never judge a book by its cover.

"Yes, I had just been released from prison on a furlough."

"What were you incarcerated for?" He had the nerve to ask me.

"No harm intended, but what the fuck does that have to do with the situation at hand? My boyfriend has almost been killed again and now my poor brother is laying somewhere in a fucking freezer. Please answer that because right now I don't have any fucking understanding. Whoever killed my brother is still out there and I can promise you the two, me being incarcerated and someone killing my brother, doesn't have any affiliation," I said catching my breath while also trying to keep my cool because I still hadn't seen the video. Damn! These muthafuckas have just turned this interview into an investigation as if I had anything to do with any of this. I set back in the chair with my arms folded across my chest with my mind going a mile a minute, trying not to lose my top.

"Just answer the question, Ms. Price. We are here to help you and to also do our job at the same time if there isn't anything wrong with that. So if you can cooperate, it would be pleasant to the department, the investigation, and to you." Detective Johnson said.

"Murder. I was arrested for murder, but I promise it doesn't have anything to do with my brother," I said instead but what I really wanted to say was fuck their prejudice ass department and the investigation because I would rather handle the shit myself, at least my family would get the justice we deserve. While the two detectives were too worried about what the fuck going on in my life, I could've been eliminating my problems.

"I knew I remembered her from somewhere," the other detective, Tate, said as if he knew me. "You were jammed up on the Graham case. You must have only done a few years because they didn't have enough evidence to convict you on murder one."

"Are you insinuating something I should be aware of, Officer? Do I need a lawyer present?" I asked curiously. I knew the type of games these muthafuckas played, especially when you played on the opposite side of the fence, but I stay awake.

"No. Not at all, Ms. Price," The other detective said, trying to interfere with me calling a lawyer. This dick head was pushing me to the edge though. "We don't have any more questions for now. But if we can proceed, it would be great. We need you to take a good look at the video and tell us if you recognize the perp." When he pressed play my undivided attention was on full effect.

As the video played, I couldn't tell at first who she could have been because her back was toward the camera. Detective Johnson fast-forwards to a better view of her face. She rushed out the door. In the right hand of the screen, you could see me and the detectives talking and shortly after they approached, I went tumbling to the ground.

The detective paused the video right on her face.

This bitch snuck in Tony's room when I stepped out! My mind was on overload and that's the reason I stepped out to get fresh air in the first place. The only time I stepped out. When I focused on her face, I swear, right hand to the sky, my heart stopped for a second. She definitely could have passed for one, but her pastel skin made the difference in their appearance. However, there were also a lot of similarities I thought.

"Could you tell us who this woman is?" Detective Tate asked. I know the truth was written all over my face.

"No, I don't know," I said nonchalantly. "Now, if there isn't anything else…" I said while taking a stand to leave. I didn't need permission. I wasn't under arrest and I hadn't done anything unethical. Yet. They would have to talk to my lawyer if they had anything else to say. "You can contact my lawyer if you have any more questions. He would gladly answer them." I made a mental note to call Robert first thing in the morning.

I walked out of the hospital surveillance room with a lot on my mind. Even if I did know who the person was on the video, I wouldn't tell them. She did look very familiar though and there is only one person who can confirm the identity of this woman. I had to find my ex-lover for the many questions that I have.

*****

A few hours later into my drive my phone started vibrating in my lap. Earlier in the hospital, I turned the ringer off because it was a distraction. My mind was already all over the place and I didn't want to say anything incriminating. Which, to be honest, I don't know how I would have when I had nothing to do with anything that has happened. But the police didn't see evidence when it came to crime, only the color of my skin and the texture of my roots.

It was now past nine o'clock as I drove absent-mindedly around the dark streets trying to clear my racing mind and heart as tears slid down my face. I'm at a point where I don't care about consequences. Fuck them! I don't know if I'm moving off impulse or if I'm in a trance maybe it's a little of both but when I looked up, I realized I was in front of CO's house. I didn't even know I knew where he laid his head, but here I was just sitting, watching, and praying. But the prayer isn't doing much for me because I had the devil standing on my left shoulder. And even though an angel sat on my right, the bad outweighed the good. If I didn't have a little conscience, I wouldn't have noticed the angel was there because the devil inside me was chanting. He spoke another lingo and I could hear him loud and clear.

My timing had been perfect. CO had just come out of his house as I got comfortable waiting. He stuck out his hand pressing the remote to disarm his car. I got out of the car without him even noticing my presence. I rushed toward him to close the distance between us, but I didn't run. Running would only make him aware of his surroundings. That could make this a fatal situation for me. I know how he gets down and trust I know he didn't mind busting his gun when necessary or beyond command.

Just when his hand reached out to open his car door, he turned toward me with a questionable look. The look of recognition was instantly written on his face. Before he could go and reach for his gun, I raised my weapon without question and fired two shots into CO's chest. The sound was louder than I had anticipated, but that didn't matter. CO fell against the car door and it held him up for a second before he slid down the door to the asphalt. I hurried to his still body checking his pulse and then his pockets. What a combination. Not because I needed the money, but just like he set my brother up, I planned to also leave his pockets turned inside out. A robbery gone bad is what they will rule my brother's case and CO's too for that matter. The only thing that matters to me was his phone. I might find something worth my while.

Out of my peripheral vision, I could see something, or someone move. When I looked to see who or what it could have been, the lights in the house on the left of me were turned off as the blinds snapped back together.

Shit, I thought. *Damn it.* Sirens. My only option is to flee. I sprinted toward my car, but not before I grabbed CO's money, jewelry, and most importantly, the phone. Of course, I left the drugs. There was no need for any of that to be in my possession.

Chapter Ten

Margeret
Something In My Heart - Michel'le

About an hour ago, CO sent me a text message stating that someone made an attempt on Tony's life by cutting his air supply but failed. I guess some things are just meant to be. I have to admit, once I left the hospital, I realized that I'd made a mistake and started to turn my car around. The reason I didn't is because shit had gone so smoothly, and it'll just be my luck that a whole army of police would be waiting to arrest me.

Desperate times call for desperate measures. It's time that I get down to business. I am willing to do what it takes to get my man back. It's like I'm caught in Charlotte's web, really more like Tony's web. I had plans to finesse this nigga by sweeping him off his feet and make him putty in my hands. Because that's what I do.

I had my dark hair pulled back off my face in a sleek pony, revealing my baby soft flawless skin. My pouty lips looked all-natural with an added touch of MAC nude lip balm. I also sported a black latex dress for the occasion. To top it off I wore a black pair of jimmy Choo peep-toe heels. I chose some simple jewelry. Diamond stud earrings and matching necklace from yours truly; Tony.

I took a look at myself in the full-length mirror even though it wasn't a requirement. I approved. I know what my man liked. He respected a lady or shall I say a boss in the streets and a freak in the sheets. Boss shit. Tonight, that's exactly what I was pulling off, lots of sex appeal. Actually, a lot of it. Too much if you ask me. I could definitely loan a few of these bum hoes some and still be the shit.

I checked my phone to see if I had any missed calls from CO. None. For a minute, I thought about how things would be if I rolled in the sack with CO, but the thought was quickly dismissed. I would've given him the hottest nigga under the sun award, but Tony took the number one spot. I would nominate him for the next runner up though.

I rubbed my belly and silently thank God that I only had a little bump because I am definitely killing this dress. I guess after all is said and done, I could still pull the baby card and see how that works out for me. I already picked out baby names and all. If it's a boy his name would be Legend. A girl? Justice.

I could hardly believe I was choosing to have a baby. Nothing came between me and my flawless body. Especially a man, but it's something about Tony that made me go against every ethical thing in my life that meant something to me. This included my sanity. But for him, I am ready to play Russian roulette. I know he is worth the gamble.

I let go of all my daydreams of Tony, for now, grabbed my Louis Vuitton clutch, and headed out the door. It is time for me to either continue to sleep with the enemy or would I be permanently putting him to sleep? For good.

Chapter Eleven

Cache
Idols Become Rivals - Rick Ross ft. Chris Rock

I finally made it back to the hospital. I decided to sit there in my car in the visitors' parking lot for a while. I need to go through CO's phone. Tonight was my lucky night. I don't know one person on this earth who doesn't have a lock on their phone besides Momo C.W. and CO. I went through his phone numbers first. I didn't see any numbers that would be connected to me or Tony, as I strolled through the many numbers he had stored.

"Damn this nigga was fucking with them hoes Peaches and Cream." I laughed. I promise them hoes will be on the front row claiming he asked one of them for their hand in marriage and that one of them is carrying his baby. Maybe even both of them hoes. *They were always dramatic*, I shook my head.

As I continued to look, I took notice of another number. It's an international number that belonged to someone in Mexico. CO had it categorized as "DA PLUG". There were several exchanges between the two, via phone calls and text messages. The first thing I thought about was one particular bitch. I know she has family ties across the border, but I also know she doesn't fuck with that side of her family. But then again, family is family. If they were anything like mine, then they are fucking with her no matter what.

Thinking back to CO and Tony's brotherhood, Tony always has been a king. Cool, calm, and collected. CO on the other hand rambunctious, rowdy, and ruthless. Their personalities were the counterpoint to the other. Boss and hitman. CO played his position well, but apparently not tonight. I caught that nigga slippin with his pants down. Fuck, what can I say? Sometimes you win sometimes you lose. Too bad for CO though because he will never get the chance to live and fight another day. Live by the gun die by the gun. And that's exactly why I have to get out of this street shit. Every time I craved the simple things in life I always get sucked right back into the belly of the beast. I didn't know when or if but if I continued fucking around my time would creep up on me like a thief in the night robbing me of my life like I robbed so many pockets before.

As I went through CO's text messages, the first one I opened was sent to the international number. It read: *someone tried to cut Tony's air supply. I'm on my way up there as we speak. That's you?*

I guess I could count CO out for that one, but I can't say he didn't get what he deserved. Fuck it. Whoever CO text right before he died is very important in all this and I needed to find out who it is. I went to his inbox next.

It read: *He dead???*

CO never got the chance to text back because he was dead before he could deliver Tony's prognosis. But bitch, he's definitely still breathing. I went over some more of their text messages from the past and took notice that CO had been hired to take someone out, but the text never mentioned who. "Maybe CO had it out for Tony all along. No way someone just woke up one day and just decided to kill their brother, but then again this is a crazy world," I spoke aloud. As I continued to read "DA PLUG" asked: *Did you handle her?*

CO: *Nah. I fumbled the ball because ya boy too busy playing captain save-a-ho.*

I looked back at the date the messages had been exchanged and realized the hit had been meant for me. "DA PLUG" I realized had to be my ex, One. It has to be her. It all makes sense to me now. The chick had to be some kind of blood related. That would explain the close similarities but then again, all Mexicans just like Chinese. There is no one in this world that despised me more than her.

Instead of continuing to play this cat and mouse game, I made up my mind to send a text message.

Me: *Really bitch? You that afraid to see me? Pull up. Had to send CO to do your dirty work? Well, right game wrong nigga. You should know what I'm about. I learned from the best.*

I put prayer hands and hashtagged it with praying for a body.

Send. I couldn't send that message fast enough. It felt like a lifetime to get my chance to dance with the devil. It finally seems like the time has come. Instantly my pressure shot up and my nerves were too bad. I became outraged as I waited impatiently for a reply to come through. What the fuck is she doing? She should have known it is me but then again, what if this isn't her and she sent someone else? Fuck, I thought shaking my head while I waited for someone, whoever to hit me back I decided to call the hospital to check on Tony.

"Baton Rouge General Mid City Medical Center, how may I direct your call?"

"Yes, could you please connect me to Antonio Clark's room please?"

"Please hold." I listened to elevator music while she attempted to connect my call.

"Hello, sweetheart," the woman said through the phone all sugary.

Is it the nurse? She wouldn't answer the phone, would she? That shit is against job regulation, huh?

"Who is this?" I asked with a sour look on my face. If only looks could kill. "Put Tony on the phone."

"Who is this? No, see that's for me to know and apparently for you to find out." She bluntly ignored my question about Tony. Immediately, I exited the car and walked briskly toward the entrance. The only thing that is unsteady about my pace or my stride was the wait for the sliding double doors to open.

"Bitch, who are you? And did One send you?" I asked ready to kill both her and fucking One.

"I assure you that I've never heard of somebody named One. I'm pretty sure whoever that may be has a government name. Oh, and by the way, the reason for my presence is strictly for my man Tony." Tony? The fuck she means her man?

"One's name is Maya Hidalgo. Do you work for her? And what the fuck you mean your man?"

"Oh, of course, he didn't give you the memo. While you were locked up, he was fucking me righteously. And he doesn't know yet, but I'm pregnant bitch." And then the phone went dead as soon as she finished her sentence.

I damn near ran but didn't want to cause attention to myself. I hope that she is still in the room because I promise whoever the fuck this hoe claims to be girlfriend, baby momma, or side bitch, I'm bout to demote her ass to nothing. Her and this baby she has alleged to be knocked up with. By the time I did make it to the room my adrenaline was pumping with such duress that my body had started to quake. I couldn't focus and the only thing in my tunnel vision was red. I refuse to continue to keep letting her defeat me.

As I rounded the corner with my hand on the gun ready for whatever, I was hit with a surprise that I wasn't ready for. Nobody was in the room. It was empty like no one was ever in the room. It had been cleaned from top to bottom. The bed was made and from the smell of the room, I can tell it had been sanitized as if it had been prepped for the next patient that would reside. I checked the nightstand drawer just in case. Nothing. His phone was also gone. I didn't know that my heart could beat as fast as it is now. My palms began to shake and sweat. My mind drifted to the people I had lost all because of me and I couldn't take it. I felt the weight of the world on my heart fuck my shoulders.

I turned and walked to the control center. I need to talk to someone.

"Excuse me, ma'am." I didn't even recognize my own voice. The receptionist threw up her pointer finger as if she was putting me on hold. Maybe she felt her phone call is just as important as me finding out what the fuck going on, but then again fuck that I'm not that type of girl. My patience is very short.

"Look, you white bitch. I need to ask you a very fucking important question," I said leaning over the counter hanging the phone call up. Stupid bitch, I thought bitterly. She just looked at me with a stale face as if I am wrong maybe I am so the fuck what?

"Where did they move my boyfriend?" I asked her.

"The nurse placed him in a wheelchair to go out for a smoke," she said afraid. I'm about to go off if I didn't hear the shit I wanted to.

"To smoke? He doesn't fucking smoke and what nurse?"

"I don't actually know her name. She said that she is a transfer from Our Lady of the Lake."

"Listen closely, I don't know what the fuck is going on here, but I suggest that you fucking tell me something different by the morning time or I'm going to kill you and then your fucking cat will die next to you."

"Was it her that came in here?" I asked, reaching for my phone. She took a look at the picture I pulled up on my phone of One.

"Yes this... this is her, but she looks a little older and she isn't this dark-complexioned," she gave me my phone back. Just what I thought, it was the same bitch that crept in here and cut Tony's air supply. She looked so much like One, that's the reason I showed her a picture of her instead. What kind of shit was going on?

If these bitches thought they'd get away with this, they had another thing coming. Killing CO was as simple for me as riding a bike and so will be the two of them. Everyone who had ever hurt me had to go. You slap me. I slap you even harder. Straight massive retaliation. For all who thought it would be easy to hurt me I will show them that thought alone had been a terrible mistake.

Chapter Twelve

Margeret
True Hurts – Lizzo

"Fuck. Fuck. Fuck." With every fuck I slapped my forehead with my open palm. How could I have been so stupid? I mentally questioned myself about my actions. Out of all fucking people, how come I had no clue these muthafuckas are connected to Maya, my niece and ex-girlfriend? What the fuck was Tony running, the playboy mansion for the circus? For the life of me, I had no clue how this bitch ended up with CO phone? She has evidence that CO and I had been partners in crime. No way was I letting her show Tony that phone. I already had a lot of explaining to do. For one I am around this bitch acting like Kathy Bates in that movie Misery where the fat white lady held that author against his will. Straight sick shit. But here I am subjected to that same shit I guess some of us just have that Kathy syndrome. Some worse than others.

"Where am I?" Tony asked, still a little drowsy from the chloroform I hit him with back at the hospital as I rolled him out in a wheelchair. Out of all the deranged things I did tonight, I must acknowledge rolling him out was easy breezy. The white nurse at the desk had been simple to entice. I caught the way she evaluated the pieces I wore like my diamonds on my wrist, the heels on my feet, and my dress. I could tell that her nine to five was only paying her bills, so I slipped mami a couple of g's to turn her head. It was nothing.

Not really sure what my plans were, I wasn't ready to face the music with Tony just yet, so I hit him with a sedative drug that I also received from the nurses' station. Ativan. That shit would knock a horse out for the count. So in seconds, that shit knocked him right out of commission. He didn't even stand a chance. Even if he was wide awake it wouldn't have mattered because I strapped him down to the chair so that he couldn't go anywhere.

As soon as I got everything squared away, I was ready to get the fuck out of the house. The mask I wore on my face had begun to itch and be sticky from the pounds of sweat. I could not breathe. I started toward the door, but as soon as my hand touched the knob, I remembered I was leaving Tony's phone. *Got it*, I thought as I turned it on. It instantly started going off like a metal detector in an airport. Of course, all messages from that bitch Cache.

"What is it that you want?" I asked as if the bitch could hear me. I really wasn't for her shit. This is between Tony and me, but if she wants it, I can definitely give. I don't mind pleasing; she can confirm this with Tony if she likes. Matter of fact, I think I'll send her just that.

Send. And wait. Not for long though because the phone indicated she was replying.

Cache: *Wrong time but we will definitely meet up. You know Cache rules everything around you.*

*****

Cache

Whoever this is claiming to be pregnant for Tony is playing fucking games as if I was an X-box. She doesn't mind pleasing? And for me to ask Tony? If his fucking ass wasn't missing in action, I would fuck him up even more than CO had.

"Hello." My phone had rung right before the message came through. I usually didn't answer unknown numbers but something in my gut told me I needed to.

"You have a collect call from *Chanel*. If you would like to accept this collect call press… one if you refuse press …" Before the operator could finish, I pressed one to accept and was connected.

"Sis, I need you to come bond me out."

"What the fuck are you locked up for?" I couldn't believe this shit was going on at a time like this.

"Bitch that white bitch from the store, she must have pressed charges because I got picked up for disturbing the peace charge. I'll give you the money as soon as I touch down, I got it in the salon. I would've been able to bond myself out, but these bitches acting like I can't do it myself."

"Money isn't the issue. Hold tight and I'm on my way," I said as I hung the phone up. I remembered back to when I got locked up all those years ago. My first time being introduced to what the parish labeled as the "pink cell" where they house women only until they were booked and processed to the back. To be honest, I was in a trance not believing I had been sent up the river on a murder charge I didn't commit.

Not even thirty minutes later I pulled up to the place I thought I would never have to return to. Thank God it's for different circumstances and it isn't me getting bonded out I had too much shit to do to be placed in a predicament like this.

After I paid the bond, I waited in the parking lot for another hour and a half until I saw Chanel appear. She wore sleep attire, so I knew they got her out of the bed. She still sashayed with pride looking like a Victoria's Secret plus-size model.

"Bitch, I owe you one," she said as soon as she climbed inside. She started digging inside her purse and she came out with some money. "If you take me to the atm I'll get the rest for you" I shook my head.

"Nah, I'm good lil sis. You know I'm supposed to be here and have your back," I said meaning every word.

"Well alright. You know I'm not going to beg you to take this money. Just don't."

"Bitch go spend that shit on some nice shoes or something."

After dropping Chanel off at home, I headed to my in-laws' house. It was late, but I was welcome at any time as long as I had breath in my body. I've been home a few months and still haven't seen my son. We've spoken via Facetime plenty of time. We also talked on the phone, but to actually be blessed with his presence hasn't happened yet. There is nothing like a hug and a wet kiss on my cheek from my baby.

For several reasons, I stopped all the beef, all the bull shit. For one nothing should ever come before my baby. Two I have no excuse for my poor parental actions and three if I died would I regret that my son never got to see me? But then again, it's not the time to speak of death I'm not dying anytime soon. There are too many things I still have to do in life that can't be accomplished in death.

Once I pulled up in front of my in-laws' beautiful equipped five-bedroom Victorian home, I cut the ignition and just enjoyed the peace. It's been a while since my mind had the chance to soak in the calmness of life. I took in the difference in the neighborhood comparing and contrasting it to where I was born and bred. I can wholeheartedly say my son and I are cut from two different cloths. Some nights or shall I say most I would go to sleep hungry. With him, that has never been the case and he could only tell you the Webster's dictionary version. As for me, it's something I lived and could give you the whole entity of the meaning of hunger. There aren't any street walkers selling pussy, sucking dick, and buying coke for a living. Here you get the best of everything: schools, parks, shopping centers, and peace at night when you are asleep. No gunshots late at night woke you up in cold sweats that left your heart racing not knowing if that bullet was meant for you but then again, they never have a name on it. That's why I love this environment for my son. Why struggle when there is no reason to be introduced to the strife?

He deserves the world and if I didn't do anything else before I expired, I would give him just that. A life of love, prosperity, and enjoyment while he's still a kid. The pursuit of happiness.

Finally, I took my keys out of the ignition and stepped out of the car. Even though this is an affable neighborhood, I know shit from sugar and didn't need anyone calling the cops because I "looked" suspicious. One thing these bitches didn't mind is phoning the boys in blue for the ones in black. Black skin that is. In a snap of a finger, they'd pull up on a bitch in no time. I'd hate to be a casualty of police brutality, so I proceeded on my mission before I was arrested for some bullshit.

*****

The next morning came too quickly for me, but I didn't mind being woken up to the kisses my son placed over my face.

"What's up, lil man?" I smiled with sleep still written across my face.

"Ma, I'm not little no more. I'm a gangsta like pops was." What could I have said to him? I just smiled and rubbed his head and kissed his forehead.

"You right gangsta, but I hope them grades are up because all the gangstas I know put them books first."

"Ma, I got this. I'm already picking the college I'ma go to and everything so that I could play ball just like pops too."

"That's right, son."

"You know I need a pair of J's to do that, huh?"

"What? You do? What about I cop you a few pairs to make sure you play ball?"

"Alright, yes! When can I come to stay with you, ma?" he asked with that same serious look on his face like his father.

"Soon son, soon." Damn, I realized I sound just like Ann when I use to beg her to take us with her. The difference though I'ma keep that promise to my baby no matter if I had to lay every muthafucka down to make sure I made it back to him alive.

Chapter Thirteen

Tony
Fatal Attraction - Kevin Gates

Things for me are looking grim. Have I been locked in this fucking room for a week or was it two? I don't know. I couldn't tell day from night anymore. Who would've ever thought a nigga like me would be held against my own will? Then on top of it all by a bitch I was fucking. Who the fuck does this shit? I should've never fucked the hoe. The time I did mix a little business and pleasure together look what happened. I know Cache was going crazy, but did she know what was really going on? Or did she fucking think I went willingly? I have been trying to get my hands untied for days, but the way that I was tied must've been joined by a boy scout. Once I get loose, I promise I'ma choke the fuck out the bitch and I don't give a fuck who she got coming behind her. The revolver that set pretty and all shiny on the table across the room told me my best bet would be to sit tight. I know this hoe is crazy enough to use it.

"What the fuck you want from me? I know it's not money," I asked trying to talk my way out of this shit.

"What do I want? Nigga, it's a little too late to be asking me that bullshit, isn't it?" She stood from the chair on the side the table where the gun rested. I was definitely kicking myself in the ass. I couldn't even be mad at her the bitch caught me slipping. I'd let my guard down. A scorned woman, but she is more than that.

"You know what this is all about Tony. Don't pretend. You know how much I hate a clueless muthafucka. If you ever thought you could fuck me and leave me, you had another thing coming. Didn't you? I may have grown up without a mother, but my father is always someone I had. I plan for my child to have the same," she said, throwing one of her legs across my lap as she placed my hand on her stomach.

"You pregnant?" I asked with my face balled up.

"Yeah … I am," she said.

"You keeping it?" I asked.

"What the fuck you mean? You should have thought of all that before you started fucking me," she shouted and slapped my face to the left side. I know her handprint was there. "That's exactly why we are where we are. You're not man enough to take responsibility."

"What the fuck are you talking about crazy bitch?"

"Crazy?"

"Fucking right. We only fucked a few times, never said shit about being together. You knew I had a girl when we first started fucking and don't play clueless. Remember you hate that shit and I do too. We had stopped dealing with each other, which is the reason I was supposed to meet your father. Why can't you just chill with all this crazy ass shit?" I shouted enough for somebody to hear.

"Typical ass muthafucka. Why the fuck you can't see where I'm coming from? *We* are family. I love you," she said crying.

"Margeret. Listen. This shit just can't happen like that. My heart belongs to someone else," I explained as she walked behind me. I could hear a phone vibrate.

"So, I see your lil girlfriend just isn't getting the picture. Tony, where the fuck are you and what's going on!" she read the text message aloud. "You know what? I have the perfect solution for her. Maybe it will help her get the picture. I tried pretending to be you through text, but this whore is very persistent."

"I don't want you and you should move on with your life," she said as she texted the message on my phone pretending to be me.

"I just can't get over you robbing and setting me up. The shit just isn't working like I thought it would. Send."

"Are you fucking serious?" I asked her. "Cache would never believe no shit like that." At least I hope she didn't anyway, but I wouldn't dare tell her deranged ass that.

"Yeah, she does actually. She just texted back. Would you like to hear it? I don't mind ya know?" She laughed as she walked back to the chair where the gun is. "Alright this is what it says," she said as she took a seat crossing her legs. "I don't know what's going on Tony, but my brother's funeral is today. I don't have time for this shit with you and this bitch. Have a nice life." She laughed like she was watching her favorite comedy show.

"Her brother?"

"Yep."

"Let me call her."

"Are you fucking serious?"

"Yeah, I am. I'll do whatever it is you want... Please." Damn, I sound like a sucker but something in my gut told me some shit just wasn't right.

"Alright," she said, surprising me.

"Alright, what?" I asked desperately.

"I'ma let you call, but we will play a little game." She walked over to me with the revolver now in her hand.

"What you doing with that?" I asked as my hands began to sweat.

"No, no, no," she said wagging her index finger. "You don't get to ask any questions, only answer. First question. Do you still want to talk to Ms. Price? Before you answer, it's only yes or no." I thought about the shit for a second as her Valentino pumps stabbed the hardwood floors.

"Yeah," I said. I have to test her because I needed to talk to Cache. Fuck it.

"Alright. Remember you chose to play. Cool?"

"Cool."

"Now, this is how we will do this … I have one bullet in this revolver. I'll give you five seconds for each pull of the trigger. I can't tell you where the bullet is placed, but you better pray that it doesn't come before you end your call." If I wasn't convinced this hoe is crazy, I definitely am now. But I'm even crazier, so I accepted.

"Make the call."

"You really love this bitch I see," she said but dialed the number like I asked her to." I'm blocking the number."

"Hello," she picked up after a few seconds of the phone ringing. I'm surprised because she never picks up on a blocked number.

"Bae," I said damn near in tears.

CLICK!

She pulled the trigger and I flinched. She balled her hand up and started her count with her fingers.

"It's me. Everything isn't what it seems. I promise."

"What you mean?" she asked, and I could tell she'd been crying.

Margaret pulled the trigger again.

CLICK!

That's twice, I thought as I counted the false shots. I was running out of time but didn't hang up, not yet.

"I'll rather not answer that right now. But what happened to your brother?" I asked ready to put money on the nigga who fucked with my family.

"CO," was all she said.

"CO?"

"Yeah, him and someone named Malik. They found CO dead too."

CLICK!

Fuck! What the fuck did I do? I hung up before Margeret could pull the trigger the fourth time. Besides, I know I didn't have much of any good luck to spare. I didn't want to push it. Then again, maybe I should have let her continue with her havoc.

"What did she say that got your dick on soft?" I just gave her the phone back. I didn't even bother answering her question. The truth was even if I wanted to, I didn't know how. All I know is I had just been added to the list of people who have hurt Cache. I just realized the night CO called me over telling me that he had someone who could lead me to One. It had been a plot all along. I killed Cache's brother without even knowing and that's a secret I would bring with me to my grave.

Yolanda Moore

Chapter Fourteen

Cache
Where the Bag At - City Girls

I wasn't any closer to finding this bitch as I was before Tony called. I knew he would find a way to call once I said I was through with him, even if it meant placing his life on the line. After making my way back to the hospital the day after I spent with my son, I found out some very valuable information. I waited in the parking lot for the nurse at the desk the night Tony disappeared from his room. She spilled everything like a cup of milk when I threatened to get her job. She begged and pleaded for me not to turn her in. She gave every excuse in the world why I shouldn't but the only plea that reached my heart was the fact that she had kids at home, and she was a step away from getting put out. I did result to kicking that bitch's ass though. I needed to teach her a very valuable lesson so now she is lying up in the same hospital where she worked. Plus, I dished the shit out to her for that attitude she carries around like she owns it.

"Sis, what good?" Klimax asked as she stepped out of her room I had slept on their couch. Chanel and Klimax not only work together, but Chanel took her in. She had found her homeless around the time I got locked up and just like my brother had turned to the streets she found security in Klimas. They'd been best friends ever since.

"Good morning," I said while headed to the kitchen to fix a cup of coffee.

"Yesterday, I went out and brought you a few things. I see you come in and out of here barely eating, sleeping, and don't even look like you breathing. After we eat, I'ma turn this bitch to a girl's spa. I'ma do your hair and nails because God those things are hideous."

"Not too much nah hoe. You know she hit." My sister Chanel came through the kitchen all loud like she usually is taking my cup of coffee straight out of my hand.

"Girl, I need to revoke that damn bond," I said rolling my eyes half-joking. "This the wrong time to be playing with a bitch coffee." I fussed but still got up to fix myself another cup.

"Y'all need to stop that shit you hoes ain't even thanked God for waking up this morning. And Chanel you already know anything you love I love even harder. As long as I'm alive Cache got me in her corner as well so you already I'ma get that ass always together."

"Fucking trader. Cache you should never trust a dick that loves dick more than you. Klimax would suck a bitch right out of a house and a home."

"Bitch you better know it. They don't call me Klimax for nothing. I can even fuck you good to have your ass tryna beat my nigga down for me fucking you so good. You'd forget Tony bitch you'd be saying Tony who?" we laughed. "Ewww bitch I don't want no faggot ass nieces or nephews walking around here," Chanel crazy-ass said like I would really let Klimax fuck me.

"Girl I might have to consider getting down with you because if you sucking dick like that you can definitely teach me something."

"Girl it's nothing I suck dick as a pass time," she said, breaking eggs then flipping the bacon in the next skillet.

"When you gone get that ring you deserve? All the good dick sucking you should be making wedding plans." Chanel said while she sat at the island drinking coffee strolling in her phone.

"Oh, trust me, my better days are out of state. I'm tired of Louisiana any damned way. These muthafuckas are the only ones who act like loving dick is a crime. Plus, I want to go and have the surgery to complete my womanhood."

"Get the fuck, are you?"

"Yep, as soon as Richard divorces his wife."

"You think he really gon' leave that bitch? You know that cracker been telling you that shit for years."

"Fucking right, he gon' let that hoe go or bitch, I'ma be locked up in Angola where the real boys are because I'ma kill that nigga. Especially because I been letting that nigga pound the round for about six months now too. And honey let me tell you, I am no joke."

"I need to introduce my new flex to that pound game," Chanel said seriously.

"Just make sure that nigga can hang with the gang because I'm telling you now that nigga gone wanna straight kill you once you put it on him."

"You bitches are too much for me," I said, taking my last sip of coffee.

"Girl so you mean to tell me as long as you been slanging that pussy over B.R you never let a nigga in the back door?"

"I didn't say that it's just y'all hoes don't mind handing your business out like insurance."

"Girl the truth is the truth and in no way can it be counterfeited. Just like my best friends" Klimax said.

"Best friends? I thought that was me," Chanel said rolling her eyes like only she could.

"You are but not when it comes to Fendi, Gucci, and Louis V." Chanel looked from Klimax to me.

"Bitch told you, you can't trust a nigga that loves dick more than you." We all laughed as Klimax fixed us a healthy plate of food.

*****

We started cleaning the kitchen and after we were done, we moved on to getting me together. I don't care what these two hoes say, call me what they like as long as I get pampered it doesn't matter. Klimax had even bought me a fire-ass Fendi dress. I didn't know why, but this hoe is up to something. She started setting my hair. From there we did make-up then nails. When everything was done, I looked and felt like a brand-new woman.

"Bitch, I needed that," I smiled.

"Anytime... I need a favor?"

"Yeah, what is it?" she had my full attention. I should've known when it comes to black muthafuckas they always had a motive.

"Before you say no just give it some thought, okay?"

"Alright, anything." The way she pampered me, I owed her.

"Remember that friend I told you about? Well, he has a client that needs a date just for a couple of hours nothing serious. Okay?" She gave me a pleading look and of course, I couldn't say no.

"Alright, but bitch this nigga bet not be gross. Beside why you couldn't get one of your people?"

"This man doesn't get down like that."

"Yo ass owes me, bitch! And here I am thinking you did all this to comfort a bitch."

"I thought after this makeover my debt would be paid in full," she laughed, applying make-up to her face.

"Hell no! You placing my ass on the market. It'll take more than a fire-ass hairstyle and dress to impress a bitch like me."

"Damn, now I see where Chanel gets that shit from. You hoes are hard to please."

Forty-five minutes later, I came out of the bathroom dressed and ready to bounce. I had to give it to Klimax. The bitch did her shit. If she didn't get down I'd have to reconsider Tony. Klimax took care of shit.

"So, bitch when are they coming to pick us up?" I asked ready to get this shit over. There was no telling what Klimax ass getting me into.

"Girl we about to drive to the Marriott and go from there.

"Alright, bitch lead the way."

When we finally made it to the Marriott we were quickly swooped up in a limo. Right then and there I knew we were dealing with muthafuckas with money. Niggas from my hood wasn't coming like this.

"Oh, this isn't nothing: my baby love giving me nice shit," Klimax read the look on my face.

We finally made it to this upscale restaurant. The type of establishment where you couldn't even pronounce the goof, you'd just paid fifty dollars a plate or more. Was Klimax ass fucking the president? I mean I have fucked enough niggas to keep a bitch laced for life but she doing it big. I ain't mad at her.

"Bitch, get that look off your face. You making a bitch look cheap like you ain't never been amongst the rich and famous. I have heard many stories about the infamous Cache."

"I would tell you to believe nothing of what you hear and half of what you see, but it'll be a waste of time."

Before I started to become irked with how late our dates were, two very tall handsome men strolled up to our table looking like NBA players. Damn! My heart dropped. It wasn't because the nigga's dick print was on display either. I had robbed his ass before.

He smiled that beautiful smile that belonged on a Colgate commercial. I hope his ass doesn't remember who I am, I thought as I smiled too.

"Hello, I'm Josiah" he greeted me by placing his hand out to accept mine. When I placed my hand inside of his I was trembling, and I hoped he didn't notice. That nigga's hands were soft just like

I remembered. Made me wonder if Richard wasn't the only one "pounding the round."

"Chanel, it's nice meeting you." Why the fuck did I give my sister's name? I hope Klimax's ass didn't put a bitch on display.

"So, Chanel," he brought me out of my thoughts once he and Richard took their seat. Alright, shit is going good so far. I doubt he remembers who I am. Wouldn't he have made it known from the jump? I guess I'll see how the night would end.

Chapter Fifteen

Margeret
Freak Like Me - Adina Howard

Look at this disgusting ass nigga sick over that nothing ass bitch Cache. I can't even play myself because disgusting or not, I still love him. That's exactly why I'm on my knees now trying to suck the life out of him right into me. I just don't understand how this one hoe got his head in the cloud. What is it that she has that I don't? How could he sit there like I'm giving him the best head he'd ever had and not think to keep me around forever?

"Fuck. Suck that shit" I was proud of myself. No matter how much Tony tried objecting me, that nigga couldn't turn down good head. Even though he didn't have much say in the matter. I still had his ass tied to the chair. I'm not stupid enough to untie his ass just yet. If you think about it, isn't it every man's dream to be tied to a chair getting his dick sucked cum sucked to life and cum again? Maybe not just pretend that's not going on and shit would be so romantic.

"I'm bout to cum... mmm uh." I stopped sucking, stood up, and slipped out of my clothes. I wondered if I should make this nigga eat my pussy since I never experienced it. I thought about it for a second and changed my mind because I didn't want to ruin the mood. Instead, I turned my back to him, took a hold of his dick, and slipped it inside me.

"You better hold that nut, nigga. Don't cum without me or I'ma kill you," I said in the heat of the moment.

"You know you gonna soon have to let me go huh?"

"What? Why are you even talking like that right now?" I asked trying to hold my composure and bust this nut that had started to build inside of me. His ass knows how to fuck up a wet dream. I started riding his dick like I was trying to get somewhere, and I was. Every few seconds I ran my pointer and middle finger across my clit. My left leg started trembling, making my legs weak, but I wouldn't dare break the rhythm.

I leaned back pressing my back into his chest as I grind my ass into his lap.

"Yes," I screamed as he sucked on my exposed neck. That shit sent me straight over the edge as we both came together. If I wasn't pregnant before this it was definitely curtains for that nigga. I came so hard that I almost freed his ass, but thought carefully about that ass-whipping he promised. He was right though. I would soon have to cut him loose, but it wasn't the right time for either of us.

*****

Hours later after injecting Tony with his usual dose of Ativan. I called the nurse over to clean him up. His wound dressing needs to be changed. I let him piss in a bucket before I doped him up but that was all I could do for him as of right now. I have also been feeding him but I'm getting bored with the shit, so I know soon I'd have to decide what I wanted to do with him. I'm not a stupid girl if I let him go, he would hunt me down until he killed me.

As I said from the beginning, I wanted to see if he was rolling with me or getting rolled over. This nigga didn't give a fuck about dying for this hoe so I guess I should just give him what it wants. A blind man could clearly see he chose her over me even over his own child.

When the nurse made it, I let her take over and that gave me a chance to go re-up on some of the things I needed. I needed a few more days just to make sure killing the father of my child would be the right verdict.

Chapter Sixteen

Tony
Cashin Out - Cash Out

"Who the fuck are you?" was the first question when I opened my eyes. I didn't notice that she had been untying me until I felt the blood flow come back into my hands. Once she got my other hand loose, I rubbed my wrist but not for long I immediately started taking the rope from my feet. I'ma kill that bitch. I don't mean to sound callous but fuck her and that child she claims to carry.

The nurse explained everything to me from the beginning all the way up to what led her to go against Margeret. Cache had given her a good ass beating once she confessed that she'd been paid to turn her head as Margeret rolled me out of the hospital. She had to go because what I had for Margeret I didn't need any witnesses.

I walked over to the blinds to see if anyone was outside or within earshot. There was no one. *Good.* I turned to see the revolver still sitting on the table. I picked it up but my impatience had turned to anger.

Please, don't kill me," she begged, sensing the anger that I felt. But it was too late to beg for salvation from me anyway. She'd do better asking God for forgiveness because I had none. Before she could get anything else out, brain matter splattered all over the wall behind her.

The streets taught me you can't trust people only greed. When she confessed to taking the money from Margeret, I knew she was only loyal to the almighty dollar. Fuck the cost of my life. She didn't even know what this bitch was capable of doing to me, but still turned her head to the bullshit.

I guess that bitch Margerret really was playing Russian Roulette with my life after all. When I opened the chamber there really weren't any more bullets. Damn. Good thing I hung up the phone when I did because I wouldn't be here to tell the story.

*****

Cache

The next morning well what I assumed to be the next morning I woke up and couldn't really remember shit. I looked over at this handsome man and that's when I remember seeing his face from the night before. I quickly jumped out of the bed when I realized who he was. Did this muthafucka drug me?

I looked around the room finding my panties and bra, then hurriedly slipping into them. I looked back over at the bed. He was still sound asleep. I started remembering a little more how Kimax and Richard left me with this fool. I recalled how I began to get light headed as he led me out of the restaurant. I knew this wasn't the time nor place to grab a cup of water, but my throat felt like I swallowed sandpaper. As I drank the water, I rubbed my neck. I began to have a flash of his hand around my throat as he rapped me. It was consent.

That's when I remembered my handbag with my gun inside. After retrieving the gun out of my bag, I straddled his lap just as he woke up. It was fine with me because I wanted his dirty ass to see my face. No matter how much I tried to remember every detail of last night I couldn't. He had to have drugged me with Rohypnol. The date rape drug better known as roofy. That was the only explanation. Memory loss, drowsiness, what else could it have been?

"I guess this is it doesn't have to be," This nigga had no clue. Maybe he really doesn't remember I robbed him. He started stroking his dick. My pussy started getting wet and it wasn't because of him. I pulled the gun from behind my back.

Boom. Boom.

"Fuck! I got blood on my bra and panties. I should've put this shit on after I killed his ass." I didn't like this color on me anyway. I'll just have to buy the same set but definitely a different color, I thought. Before I cleaned myself and got the fuck out of there.

Yolanda Moore

Chapter Seventeen

Maya
Trap Queen - Fetty Wap

In a world that can be cold, harsh, violent, and brutal at times humanity proves just the opposite. Over the last few years, I have become a vet in this here dope game and it doesn't owe me shit. I haven't even hung up my gloves yet. I was nowhere near it. My grandfather has made sure of that. Just like he had done with my mother so many years ago. Speaking of my mother, since I've been here, I've felt closer to her than I've ever felt in my life. Plus, she was the sole purpose of me coming here, for revenge.

When my mother, the Hidalgo princess was formally introduced to the game it wasn't something she craved. We were opposites in that category because I've always wanted money, power, and more money. Fuck respect because as long as you had money muthafuckas respected you. Look at Trump. How the fuck his idiotic ass make it in the White House? Money. Because I don't know no muthafucka that stupid that gains respect without righteousness. But then again what's that saying? Righteousness is only for the wicked.

Anyway, back to the money. I get those yearnings from my father's side of the family. Born and raised in negligence so what's expected but hunger? With that said my grandfather assured me that my "dead beat" father, his words not mine, didn't mind my mother crowning him king and giving him the keys to the streets.

My grandfather confessed to me that he didn't like what my mother had done one bit, but he assured me that never would he ever harm her or my father for that matter because that's how much he loved my mother. I was always taught that the eyes never lie and something in my soul told me my grandfather spoke the truth. Now on the other hand I know he is withholding some very valuable information and I do plan to get it out of him. Voluntary or involuntary. However, he wanted to do it. I know for facts my mother and father died under this roof and even though shit was sweet for me I still needed answers.

"Good morning, grandfather," I said walking out the patio as he smokes his favorite Cuban cigar. "When are you going to give them stinky things up?" I smiled wrapping my arms around his neck kissing his cheek. "How many times do I have to tell you that they are bad for you?"

"As many times as it will take. I told you, I don't plan to give them up. I'm taking them to the grave." I laughed because the sad part about it is that he was serious.

"Alright, but don't be like I should've listened," I laughed. I liked this someone I can relate to feel free to joke with and have that family bond and actually share the same blood. I thought as I let the wind blow my hair.

Without saying anything, my grandfather got up and went inside, but returned shortly after with a few photo albums and a DVD.

"I want to show you something," he said, taking his seat. I didn't say anything, I just waited for him. He opened the first album it was pink. Must've been my mom's. The first photo was of my mom right here on this same patio smiling up at whoever was taking the picture. I assumed it had to be my father because only someone you're in love with could make you glow like my mother in this picture.

"Here is where your mother fell in love with your father. I loathe the fact that my daughter had found security in another man. That only made me actualize the fact my baby girl had grown up. From the day she was able to talk, I took her under my wing. For whatever reason, I just wasn't blessed with a son. But that was ok with me as long as my legacy would remain in the hands of someone that carried my blood."

"Why didn't you choose T. Margerret?" I asked. Placing the T. on Margerret's name left a bad taste in my mouth, but out of respect for my grandfather, I swallowed the vomit that dared to come up every time I thought of her.

"Well, sweetie that's a long story." *Nigga, I wanna know. This could play a big part in all this,* I thought.

"I'm not going anywhere," I said letting him know I didn't give a fuck about him making excuses.

"Alright. I guess I owe you at least the short version." If I had big floppy ears like a dog, they would definitely stand straight up along with a wagging tail. "Margerret isn't my daughter," he said as he hung his head.

"WHAT?!" It just came out like that I didn't mean to sound all hard up. "How?" I asked.

"I don't want you to think any different of your grandmother."

"I don't even know her." Damn. I didn't mean to sound so harsh it just came out that way. Fuck it, what's done is done.

"She cheated on me with my best friend, my right hand." Muthafucka.

We just got all kinda scandals going on around this bitch, I thought.

"Since I let you know all of this, I guess I should tell you the rest."

"The rest? It's more?"

"Yeah. Margaret is your mother, and our father is your father. Before you go ludicrous take this DVD." That same numb feeling you get when the dentist shoots you up with Novocain? Well, that's exactly what I felt; paralyzed.

"I thought you said you only wanted family doing business?" I said. Even though I was still in shock I still worried about the crown.

"That's true, but sometimes even bosses go against the grain. And I know a good hustler when I see one. Welcome to the family, Maya. You were born an original. Don't die a copy." He stood, kissed my cheek and walked off. I guess he had finished talking.

I stayed in that same spot on the patio thinking about every fucking thing I ever stood for. It was all lies. I needed something to clear my head and busting a nut just wasn't it for me. I looked over at the Cuban cigars my grandfather left and lit one up. Was it still ok to call him my grandfather?

I looked down as I took a puff of the cigar finally remembering the DVD, he gave me. I went to my quarters to see what the disc held. I placed it in the player pressed play and waited until it loaded.

A'nett. Why was she on here and who was recording this? I didn't have to speculate long. Margaret. *I should've known*, I thought, paying close attention to every detail. That's when I took notice of the clothes A'nett had on. She was dressed in the same clothes the day she committed suicide. Tears began to rapidly fall from my eyes as it hit me. The truth was right here in front of me, caught on DVD.

Margerret had staged the whole thing. A'nett didn't commit suicide. She had been murdered... by my... mother.

Chapter Eighteen

Tony
Dilemma - Nelly ft. Kelly

"Cache, pick up the fucking phone, ma," I said to myself as I paced the floor on the side of the dead body. I had decided to wait only a few minutes for Margerret to come back because I was ready to dead that bitch too. The wait was over. There is no one besides Cache that I left breathing that could tell the story of fucking me over and got away with it. But Margerret is a whole other story. She won't get that same entitlement. If I had the time to wait on this bitch, I would wait a lifetime for her to return just to send that bitch to meet her maker. But I couldn't, the cops are closer than they were ten minutes ago.

"Fuck," still no answer. The voicemail picked up again. Maybe she didn't pick up because of this off-brand ass number. I snatched the phone from the nurse I'd just killed, she won't be needing it where she's going. Besides, that bitch Margerret took my phone with her. I looked around the house quickly to see what I can utilize to destroy any evidence of me ever being in the domain. I walked into the living room and realized I was in the home of the nurse I left lying in the room where I had been held captive. This bitch really played a major part in all of this. Knowing that made me feel even better for knocking her ass off. A picture on the mantel caught my eye. She and I will assume the three children were hers. Yeah, my heart went out to the kids, but they won't be the first to not have a parent present and won't be the last. I carefully placed the picture back where it came from and continued on my search to ravage my existence.

Walking out the back door spotted a shed. I looked to see if anyone would see me when I came into view of the blistering heat.

Nope. A wooden fence had been built around the entire backyard for privacy. Either keeping someone from leaving or coming in as they would please.

I didn't have to look much longer. I located exactly what I would need to put this shit behind me and not allow it to bite me in the ass later. Sitting on the side of the blue and white shed sat a red gas can. Today was just my lucky day because there was enough fuel to embark on a wildfire in a forest.

Walking back into the house I started dispensing gas from the back door all the way up to the corpse. I looked around for a lighter or even a box of matches.

"Fuck! Are you serious?" I then ran to the kitchen once I finally found it. Twisting a piece of newspaper, ignited the stove and lit the tip of the paper how my moms used to when turning the oven or fireplace on. I briskly walked back to the room praying that the fire from the paper didn't go out or worst fall on the trail of gasoline. When I made it to the doorframe, I dropped the fire before it went out. I jumped back before the shit went up in flames. EMT would be discovering two bodies instead of one.

I snatched the keys to her car and rushed out the door. As soon as I pulled out of her gravel driveway, I began calling Cache number back.

"Hello," she asked out of breathing. What the fuck is she doing?

"Where the fuck you at?" I asked, jumping to conclusions. Even though I love her, I'll never forget her past.

"Tony?" I couldn't tell if it was a surprise or a question in her voice.

"Yeah, bae. Where the fuck you at?" I repeated myself as I tried keeping control of the car as the cops headed into the direction I had just come from.

"I need you to come get me. I got caught up in some shit."
Caught up? I thought what the hell had she gotten herself into while I've been gone?

"Alright. Say no more and give me your location."

"I'm at the Marriott."

"Which one?"

"The one by the casino. I'ma be ducked off on the side of the bank by the Smoothie King. You might not recognize me, but I have a baseball cap on baggy clothes with a pair of black shades."

"Alright. I love you."

"Love you." I hung up just in case she was caught up in some shit that would have a tracker placed on her phone. I was like thirty minutes from her destination, but I floored the gas because I knew she needed me more than ever. I wasn't about to let her down fuck that.

When I made it downtown there were police cars everywhere like in that movie *21 Bridges*. I couldn't even drive anywhere near the bank, so I hopped out of the car. I took the quarters from the console dropping them in the parking meter. I didn't know how long it would take me to find Cache, but I wasn't leaving until I did. I rushed through the crowd of people trying to stay concealed by the jungle.

"Everyone needs to stay back. You can't cross the yellow tape," an officer said trying to keep the crowd away. After this circus, we will definitely be going back on lockdown. Just the other day the governor stopped the state from moving into phase three of the COVID pandemic!

"I'm right here," I heard Cache's voice as her hand touched the lower part of my back.

"Damn," I said barely recognizing who the hell she was. I grabbed her hand, leading her back toward where I parked the car.

Once we got in the car and she started telling me her story, I couldn't even be mad. I looked over at her as she looked out the window with both of her feet propped on the dashboard. I grabbed her hand and squeezed it. I knew right then and there I wanted to be with her for the rest of my life, even if the rest of my life ended tonight by the bullet of a cop.

It is impossible to divide love. True love only knows how to multiply. I never thought I could love anyone as much as I did her. I realize the engagement ring I bought was still tucked safely in my pocket. It was either now or never. I may never get this possibility again. I went inside my pocket and pulled out the ring I bought just for this moment. As crazy as it may seem, this is just as special as if I got down on one knee.

I used my knee to help steady the driver's wheel and slid the ring on her finger. She looked over at me and smiled without saying a word. Nothing was required. We both knew that Cache Ruled Everything Around Me.

Chapter Nineteen

Chanel
Outside Today - Youngboy

Boom. Boom. Boom.

"Who the fuck is it? Beating on my fucking door like the damn police," I said snatching the door open. I started down the barrel of a gun. Behind it stood two detectives. One white and the other black.

"Put your fucking hands up!" they yelled as they bagged me up into my living room with my red teddy on.

"What the fuck is going on? You have the wrong address!" I yelled just as loud but knew I needed to shut the fuck up when an officer the streets called Brah Stupid pointed his gun. There would definitely be some police brutality in this bitch if I didn't.

"Where is Cache Price?" he asked me.

"I don't know," I said looking him in the eye. They say when you look a dog dead in the eyes, it made them bitches tuck their tail and back down. I guess that shit only happens with a man's best friend because in human form the shit didn't work. If it did or not, I'll never give my sister up even if I did know her whereabouts.

"So, you wanna play that game?" Brah Stupid got in my face. Before I knew it, he'd smashed the butt of his gun on the side of my temple and I swear ass went flying any and everywhere. But that shit was the least of my worries.

"Brah, what the fuck or you doing? This shit is being recorded on the body cam."

"Fuck all that shit, Tate. If you thought this shit would be a playground, you should've stayed patrolling the schoolhouse." Brah Stupid turned back toward me trying to rip my clothes off.

"Get the fuck off me you white muthafucka!" I screamed, kicked, and clawed. *I wished Klimax hadn't gone with Richard and would've stayed home with me,* I thought as tears slid down my face.

"Man, come on here," Detective Tate called pulling Brah stupid off me. Brah Stupid spun around forgetting about me for a second drawing his gun on Detective Tate.

Boom. Boom.

Everything happened all at once. Brah Stupid fell on the side of me. Detective Tate put two shots in his chest before his life had been taken from him. Everyone knew in life it always came down to you or me. And in this case, the greatest man prevailed. The question in this matter though, is would Detective Tate be acquitted like every other cop in his story? Or would this be another black man that will fall victim to enslavement to the white man?

*****

Klimax

"Here is a cigarette and a coke," the detective who introduced himself as Johnson said as he slid the coke, cigarette, and lighter toward me. I picked the lighter and cigarette up first. Fuck the coke for now. I crossed my legs sitting sideways in the chair with one arm cross as it steadies the hand that held the now lit smoke.

"What can you tell me about the night you last seen Cache with Josiah?"

"Not much. I was too busy sucking dick," I said knowing he only pretended to not like trans. I knew my type of nigga.

"If you can keep that volatile talk to yourself, it would be highly appreciated," Johnson said as he eyed his partner who hasn't taken the time to introduce himself.

114

"Cool. Whatever you want Mr. Officer." Letting that nigga know he could pull me over like that boy Lil Wayne.

"Do you have an alibi?"

"Yes, I just told you I had a mouth full of dic… I mean yes." I looked down in my purse and came out with Richard's business card. Yes, boy! I snatched me a stockbroker off Wall Street.

"Alright. Ma'am. I mean sir you can go but we will be calling this Mr. Richard to confirm your testimony of your whereabouts."

"If that's all officers, here is my card with my information on it. If there is anything else, I can help you with don't hesitate to call me," I added emphasis on anything as I eyed Detective Johnson sliding my card to him… only. Fuck I know I'll be bagging Richard's richy-richy ass soon, but that doesn't mean a girl can't start the bachelorette party early?

I walked out of the precinct and waited on the curb until my uber came. I hope I didn't look like a hooker but then again…

Not long after, my Uber pulled up and I made a mental note to give them a five-star rating because one thing a bitch hated was waiting. The window rolled down just a little and the voice inside said for me to get in the front seat.

Maybe I shouldn't get in at all. This could be the green river or the craigslist killer. I guess I'll just have to see, I thought as I stepped off the curb into the front seat.

To my surprise, it was Mr. Officer pulling me over. I was definitely about to suck his dick for all it was worth. Maybe he'd forget about looking for Cache. Maybe.

*****

Margaret

Every saint has a past, and every sinner has a future. This statement is considered cliche and yet it is one of the greatest truths. I felt it was my time to prevail. To conquer. To rule. When I got back on the road to where I held Tony captive, the whole fucking block looks like it was up in flames. *Maybe I left the stove on or something*, I thought for a second. Hopefully, I did. Fuck it, I'll find another father for my baby or let Tony's family deal with the kid like I did with Maya all those years ago.

I didn't feel bad about what I did. I was too young to be a mother any damn way. She should be glad I didn't abort her ass instead. Did that at least make me have a heart?

I called the Baton Rouge Metro Airport and booked me a flight out tonight to head back to my home. I could taste the Tequila and Bean burritos as we speak.

Chapter Twenty

Cache
Guadalajara, Mexico
Six Months Later...

Gunwalk - Lil Wayne ft. Juicy J

"Moms," my son called out to me. I was sitting on the beachfront of my home located in Guadalajara, Mexico sitting in the sunbathing in glorious heat with my big floppy hat on, when my baby grabbed my attention. My mind was deeply rooted in a novel by the legendary Cash *Thugs Cry.*

"Yes, my baby?" I smiled, looking up from the book as it rested on my pregnant belly.

"Whoever killed my dad I want them dead. When I grow up I'ma kill whoever killed him" Knasir said with so much venom as he went back to playing his PlayStation as if he hadn't just threatened to take a life or was it a promise? I was shocked to hear that kind of talk come from my son. Where did he get that shit from? Had his grandparents told him what happened to his father? Was Knasir tired of hearing the story of God taking knowledge to heaven?

There was no question or doubt about what needed to be done, what had to be done... to save my child. I didn't want him to ever feel like he had to take on the responsibility of his parents like I had done with my own. I should have just killed Maya a long time ago. I had no excuses. The bitch shouldn't still be breathing. I fucked up. I know I did. Knasir shouldn't have thoughts of murder. I had to get this taken care of and quick if for no other reason to ease his mind would alleviate mine. Just the thought of knowing my baby boy could sleep peacefully at night made all the difference.

*****

The night in the sky told a story of its own as I made my way around the back of the Hidalgo compound with murder on my mind. This is the same place where A'nett lost her life. Where they claimed she committed suicide, but I know the truth from the lie that had been told to me. A suicide note. That shit was way beyond A'nett to do something so anal. She loved us too much to leave especially when she had her whole life ahead of her. Not when things would've surely gotten better. I know that I had left them when things were unbalanced. We had just lost our mother, so I understood. I know things were hard, it was on all of us. Everything had fallen upon me, so I had inherited the responsibility of my mother. A responsibility no one else wanted. I wasn't even sure how to be a mother myself. At the time, I thought money was the most important thing to keep a smile on their face. When you can't rub two pennies together that's where you lose yourself, trying to fill those big holes up with materialistic things. I was wrong. All the money in the world couldn't stop the inevitable, a prison sentence. I couldn't rob, steal, fuck or manipulate myself out of doing time. This only in return taught me the values of life: patience is a virtue. I never knew the quality of life until I couldn't live anymore and everyone around me dictated the way I dwelled.

As I ducked and dodged every spotlight staying as close to the dark corners, I spotted an armed guard, sleeping on his post. I crept quietly upon him, pressing the silencer to the back of his head, and squeezed the trigger.

Psst. And just like that, he'd sleep eternally now. I took his AK 47 and tossed it in the pool. Big guns make too much noise and I didn't come here to start an orchestra. I only came to sing lullabies.

I had no clue where this bitch slept in this big ass house, but I was determined to kill her tonight. I wouldn't have it any other way, I thought as I stumbled across a library. I slipped inside for reasons unknown to me, but I went with my move. Maya had really done well for herself. I thought as I looked around the room. I don't understand rich muthafuckas. They bought all this nice ass expensive ass shit and did nothing with it. There are so many rooms here. I know it's been years since anyone has stepped foot in some of them.

I looked around and tried to feel A'nett in this room. Did she come here to read? Just when I began to get lost in my thoughts, I notice a glisten from my peripheral. When I walked over to the entertainment center, it was only a DVD. I picked it up and held it in my hand for a while. I couldn't help myself, but they say curiosity killed the cat, and tonight the cat isn't the only one who'd be killed by curiosity. I took the DVD carefully out of its clear case and slide it into the DVD player.

Loading…

The TV came to life and across the screen came the face of the mystery woman who had cut Tony's air supply at the hospital. For the moment, I was stuck in a trance as goosebumps covered my body sending a chill throughout.

She moved across the room and there across the bed laid A'nett. What the fuck? My mind began to race as well as my heart. Tears began to rapidly race down my face as I watched the truth unfold in front of my own eyes. There is nothing or no one that could convince me differently.

"Oh my God. Cache… I'm sorry." I spun around on my heels, gun drawn immediately as I had taken a protective stance ready to pounce at any moment.

"I didn't know… I swear…"

Psst. Psst. Psst.

Maya's body fell backwards with each bullet that hit her chest cutting off her pleading words.

*****

"Ahhh I screamed as I woke up in a cold sweat with my gun in my hand, realizing I was only having a dream.

"It's ok, Cache. It was only a dream." Tony rubbed my back trying his best to comfort me. I didn't respond to his gentleness. This being a dream is what upset me. I needed to kill her before it drove me crazy or sent me into labor. I pulled the covers from over my legs to get out of the bed and headed to the kitchen to get a glass of water.

"The truth isn't only a dream," I said softly to myself as I fixed a glass of water. Just like this mystery woman had come to pass this dream would too because in my heart I know A'nett had been murdered.

"Bae are you good?" Tony came behind me wrapping his arms around my waist. "What about my baby?" He rubbed my protruding belly.

"Yeah, we're good." I turned in his arms to look into his handsome face as I leaned against the sink.

"Are you sure?" He kissed the tip of my nose.

"Yeah," I answered. At least I will be when I destroy everything that meant me no good.

Death is not the greatest loss in life. The greatest loss is what dies inside us while we live…

Chapter Twenty-One

Tony
502 Come Up - Bryson Tiller

After Cache fell back to sleep, I had to get out of the house. I hated when she cried that meant that I needed to step my game up because there is something that I wasn't doing correctly. My mind was all cloudy and fucked up and being out in the middle of nowhere didn't make it any better. No lie the weed was alright, but it couldn't fuck with the shit I got from my Jamaican friends. Down here these muthafuckas aren't only known for cheap labor, but also good coke and hiding in plain sight. As I was saying though, out here hiding out is for the birds. Something had to give. I did not know how to tell Cache that I was broke. We both were broke as fuck. If only I could get back to the states. The money is galore there if I could get my fucking hands on it. But with the cops on our back like backpacks, it will be like solving a murder mystery that turned into a cold case. But until then I was going to rock out with my cock out. Nobody said it better than Jay Z. "It's a million ways to get it, so choose one."

With Cache sleeping like a newborn baby, I decided to hop inside the car we owned and just drove through the dark streets. I had no destination in mind so before I knew where I was, I found myself parked across the street from a nightclub. It is known to be frequently used by tourists and from the outside looking in the place seemed to have money. A nigga is determined to get a piece of the pie. I couldn't believe I am about to subject myself to the same bullshit I criticized Cache for once or twice if I admit the truth. No lie, in this moment I understood her strife and just as quickly as I had once pointed the finger is just as quickly as "by any means necessary," had become my motto. I am ready to do whatever it took to take care of me and mine. *Damn*, I shook my head. "How the tables have turned," I said aloud.

Before I could change my mind, I checked the Glock that set on the passenger seat rolling with me like a true ride-or-die bitch. With the safety off and a bullet relaxing in the chamber begging for a body, I decided there was no better time than now to go with my move. I eased out of the car like a thief in the night while slipping the hood of my jacket over my head making myself as inconspicuous as possible.

When I made it to the door, posted in the front was a Mexican that looked like a killer. I knew right then and there this place wasn't to be fucked with and I didn't want to let my guard down. Fuck that shit though. I wasn't about to get caught slipping. A nigga made it too far to get banged by a wet back.

After paying my admission without being I.D.'d, I made my way through the club. It was dimmed just enough for me and I spotted the perfect table for me to duck off and not be seen.

There were a few bitches walking around in nothing but G-strings and heels with titties that set at attention. With all the bitches in here put together I know they'd paid a few grand to get a nigga dick hard. If I must admit myself it was money in this muthafucka and I was about to pocket some of this shit.

Even though I am surrounded by a bunch of bad bitches I know the illusion they were trying to create. But if you weak you beat and I'm just not that type of nigga to get got. Most of these muthafuckas had their head in the cloud and these bitches walked around draped in these niggas life's saving. Now tell me where they do that at?

As I continued to look around and scope the place out. It definitely didn't take a rocket science to peep the shit that was going on. For every man that walked through the side door, a woman followed closely behind.

"How can I help you?" I was caught off guard by a sugary voice because I was so engrossed in the scene that played out in front of me. When I turned and looked toward the voice that grabbed my attention, I was met by a sister. The first one I've seen all night.

"Actually, you can." I smiled mischievously as if she would get it.

"Ok, I'm pretty sure whatever it is you are looking for we carry it in every shape, form, or fashion… color and flavor," she spoke flirtatiously.

"Aight," I smiled. "I would love a hot, tall glass of chocolate," I said licking my lips, testing my theory.

"Alright. Follow me," she said, not even telling me her name and not requesting to obtain mine. That shit was cool with me because if she would have asked, I would have told her some bullshit. I guess they respected client privacy.

With my hands still tucked tightly in the pockets of my hoodie, I pretended not to pay anyone else no mind. Before we went to behind door number "one", we stopped at the door to pay a fee. Good thing I came strapped with a little change. Even though it took everything I had in my pockets, I didn't trip because I am definitely going to make a dollar out of fifteen cents.

Once we were branded with a glow-in-the-dark stamp, the bouncer let us inside. The first thing I noticed was that there is definitely a different type of hype than on the other side of the door from where I just come through. I *ain't mad at cha*, I thought giving whatever muthafucka who thought of this shit props. This shit had to be a multimillion-dollar business.

Upon entering the back there were several rooms off on each side. Right in front of us down the hall, I could see a room that was dressed up to be a lounge. From where I stood, I could see a smoke gray sectional with three occupants. Two women and one man. One lady locked eyes with me right before snorting coke off the table with a crooked smile plastered across her face.

In that instant, I quickly took an evaluation of the situation at hand. Before I learned to be the suave nigga that I am today, I used to be this fool. Lots of money and everybody should know where there is money, there are hoes, in addition to the two more problems.

In a twinkling moment, I knew his ass would be all the answers to my problem solving. As soon as the "nameless" chick and I stepped through one of the side rooms, she was on a nigga like a fat bitch in a Little Debbie factory.

"Woah, woah, lil momma. What you doing?" I asked when the first thing she did was hit her knees.

"What? What, did I do wrong?" She looked as if she had done something wrong. "You want a golden shower or something? Should I pull out the strap to fuck you with?"

Before that shit was out her mouth good, I drew my pistol with no hesitation.

"If your fucking ass come near me with any of the shit you just named, I swear I would kill you and every muthafucka in here for allowing some shit like that to go on," I said as I covered her mouth holding my piece to her head. No, I did not plan to kill her but muthafuckas respected fear before love, and if that is what this shit had to result to then so be it. But don't get it twisted, I would knock a nigga or a bitch off if a threat presented itself.

"Wait, daddy," she pleaded, throwing her hands up and shielding her face as if that gesture would be enough to stop the type of pressure I was pushing and the pain I would cause if this bitch played any of them sick-ass games.

Like I said, more money more problems. Muthafuckas with money all ways doing stupid shit. "Paying for a bitch to fuck you in the ass is going too far. But to each its own. I don't get down like that lil momma. And if any bitch thought about pissing on me, they got another thing coming," I said placing my gun back at ease.

"What did you come for?" she asked, still frightened. As she spoke, I took a seat on the edge of the bed.

"For the same fucking thing you did. Money. And I'm ready to fuck whoever out of it to get it. The only difference between you and I, is there won't be any sexual exchange ma. But I got plenty of physical discomfort for anyone who doesn't mind dying."

"Listen," she pleaded from on her knees. I had to admit that shit made my dick jump. Fuck, I'm still a man at the end of the day, but I also wasn't stupid. I knew if Cache ever found out I even thought of another bitch in a sexual way she would cut my dick off.

Instead of responding verbally, I gave her my undivided attention because I heard something in her voice. Maybe even desperation.

"I'm too fucking young to die and whatever the fuck you need me to do I'm down. Plus, my ass just started working here and I plan to head back across the border. I'm not making enough money any fucking way. So, I'm down for whatever if you put me on." I thought about that shit for a second and the more I evaluated the situation the more I realized that she had much more to offer than sex.

"Aight," I said thinking of exactly what it is I need her to do.

I began to look at her in a new light trying to place the pieces together where she would fit on the chessboard.

Yolanda Moore

Chapter Twenty-Two

Tony
That Iron – Boosie, Beelow, Juvie

"Alright, check this shit out," I said hoping that I wasn't making a mistake that I would regret. From this point on though it was either do or die. I had already let this bitch into my world, and I couldn't turn back now.

"Do you know the person that I locked eyes with when we first stepped behind the door after paying to enter?" I asked praying she did. His ass looked like a big fish.

"Yeah, that is one of the top-paying customers. He has inquired about me a few times, but I have heard rumors about all the freaky shit he likes to do and I'm not pressed to get down with the shit he's doing," she said shaking her head. I just looked at her with a look on my face that said, "bitch please."

"Whatever that muthafucka want, you give it to him. Aight? I know whatever that nigga want on demand and supply should get no worse than hittin' a nigga with some plastic or pissing on his ass. Plus, if you go all the way through with this you can head back to where you come from and never look back." she looked at me as if she wasn't too sure if she wanted to go through with what we have already shook on.

Ole girl did not know it, but we had both crossed that line and this shit was either get down or lay down, but I was not going to let her just up and leave this room especially knowing what I came to do. Who is to say she wouldn't run her ass out this bitch and try to get paid for the information and turn me over to the muthafuckas I planned to hit?

"I'm ready. Just tell me what I need to do," she said after thinking about what I said. Immediately I began to run the plan down to her. She told me after I finished talking how much of a big spender he is. I took everything she said into consideration and was ready to put my plan in motion.

She, who I found out was D'zyna, slipped out of the room we occupied. She walked out with more confidence than she had just a second ago.

Hours had passed since I left the house, which caused me to pull out my phone because it hadn't vibrated since I was gone. Cache usually knows when I have left the bed from the lack of my warmth. She must have really been tired because when I looked at my phone, I still hadn't gotten a call from her. If she was up, she would be blowing my shit up trying to figure out where I was.

Like I said, my family is my sole purpose for being out committing a crime. Plus, I had too much pride as a man to tell my woman that we were broke and if I didn't do something soon, we would be not only wanted by the law but out on our ass.

I looked at the time once more as I came out of my thoughts of home to focus on the task at hand. I didn't need to be distracted once it was time to put in work. I told D'zyna that I would give her at least twenty minutes to get them other hoes out the room and to have dude's dick deep in her throat by the time I came in with my pistol in hand. That time had come and as I peeped out of my room into the hallway there was not a person in sight. Good. If you asked me, shit was going too good for it to not be a trap at the end of it all but being that my desire outweighed all else I continued to go with my move without thinking twice.

I staggered down the hall as if I had too much to drink. My hands continued to rest in my pockets on the trigger of my gun just in case a muthafucka bust the wrong move. I would pop off before they even realized what happened to their ass.

Two doors down from my destination out walked a woman with small tits which were the first I had seen around here. I guess she did not have a complex about her chest, but I could definitely tell she still spent her money well. She literally had an ass that looked like a shelf and if I had a glass I would most def test the theory and set my glass on her ass.

"Damn daddy. Are you alright?" she asked, placing her hand on my chest. I did not answer, I just continued to perform being drunk. I played that shit well by slapping her hand and grumbling something incoherent. I did not even understand, so I knew she didn't either

Without missing a beat, I kept walking, but I didn't miss what she said, and it went something like this. "I gotta keep an eye on his fine ass because I could easily hit that nigga up without sucking his dick. The drunk ones are my favorite."

If I didn't know any better, I would've thought she was talking to someone else, but I guess it was a mental note to herself to catch my ass slipping before I slipped through the cracks. All I gotta say is I wish a bitch would like a kitchen cabinet. She can fuck up and think she can fuck with a nigga, but she got the game twist. Like my grandmother used to say: never underestimate a desperate muthafucka because they would leave you tied and twisted in the bottom of an ocean. Trust me when I say I'm that "desperate muthafucka" she spoke about at this moment.

With just only a few more steps I realized that I had made it to my destination. I transformed into an alter ego I didn't even know I had, and I decided at that moment to call him Malachi. The first name that popped in my head.

"I am him," I whispered before I busted into the door, gun held high, as if I did this shit for target practice.

"Oh my God," D'zyna and the crew screamed just as I kicked the door closed with my right foot. I didn't expect there to be a third person because I told this muthafucka to clear the room of everyone besides her and him.

Well, no need to cry over spilled milk, I thought without missing a beat.

"Get the fuck on the ground!" I yelled pointing my gun at these faggot ass niggas. D'zyna had already put me on about the soundproof walls they had installed in the rooms because of all the freaky shit they did. Sometimes these sick ass muthafuckas paid to get their ass beat, and this bitch was no different.

Homeboy did what I commanded, but the other nigga and D'zyna ignored me. D'zyna came from under her silk teddy with a small handgun instead, pointing it directly at his dome right after placing a bullet in the chamber. She surprised the fuck out of me and that made me make a mental note to not take my eyes off this bitch.

"You fucking heard him. Do as he said or I'ma crack your fucking skull and spill your brains over the expensive ass suit you paid entirely too much for," she said flicking her wrist toward the floor letting him know where to go. His ass didn't get it so she came above her head with her gun and came down with a force that sent his ass straight to where she politely asked him to go the first time.

"Yeah, I gotta watch this bitch," I whispered under my breath.

"You said something?" she asked looking at me with a smile plastered across her face.

"Shit, no. Now let's get this money so we can bounce."

Instantaneously, we had everything plus more than I had come for. We had to flip the room upside down to get the shit because these two homosexuals were too geeked up on coke to realize what was really happening. I think they thought we were roll playing and that shit was fine with me.

"Ready?" I asked looking toward D'zyna making sure that we left nothing untouched or unturned.

"Yeah," she said as we headed for the door once the two men were tied up. There was no reason for me to head back to the room

I was in, so I headed to the door that leads back to the bar area, hoping the bouncer didn't realize that I didn't enter with the bag.

"Meet me outside across the street. I don't want us to walk out together. Aight?" I said ready to get the fuck out of here as soon as possible. She gave her head a slight head nod and we went our separate ways for the time being.

*****

Not even five minutes later, I spotted D'zyna briskly walking across the street toward me when she hopped in the car. I didn't waste any time pulling off.

She directed me to the hotel room she had been staying in. When we made it there, we went straight into her room grabbing the duffle bag as well.

When we entered the room, I had to take a double-take at her. She was covered in blood like she had just committed a massacre, but I knew that there wasn't that much blood when I left the room so what the fuck happened when I left the room?

"What?" she asked, noticing the look on my face.

"What the fuck happened from the time I left you?" I was not sure if I really wanted to know.

"I could not leave them muthafuckas alive," she said, straining her voice as if I should get her reason for her actions and I should. I guess I just didn't expect any of this from her. "They knew me, not *you*. If the shoe was on the other foot, you would do the same thing. So, don't judge me," she said right before walking off to the bathroom to get cleaned up.

"Damn," I thought. I'm really fucked if Cache finds out about this shit. I always attracted the crazy bitches. I shook my head thinking if Cache and D'zyna ever ran across each other they would create a storm worse than hurricane Katrina.

By the time I got everything separated evenly, D'zyna was headed out of the shower draped in only a white plush towel on her head and wrapped around her body.

As soon as my dick jumped for the second time from seeing her, my phone began to vibrate. I didn't have to look down to know who it was hitting me up. Cache. It was like she could sniff me out when I thought about giving the d' away. Instead of answering, I let it ring. I knew I had some explaining to do later, but for now, I would ride the wave. While D'zyna was inside the bathroom, I came up with an idea on how I could get me and Cache back across the border without being touched. Honestly, I should've been thought of this, but I don't really know how the shit would turn out.

If I had to die for Cache and the kids to live, then so be it but I knew this shit had to be done. There is only one person on this side of the battlefield that I knew had enough connections to help get them, alphabet boys, off our ass. Emilio Hidalgo.

The more I thought about it the more it made sense to me. If Margerret told her father anything about what happened between us I would not be alive today to tell the story no matter if she was in the wrong or not. Plus, I would like to know if she was really pregnant with my child. If so, this would be around the time of the birth of my first child.

Chapter Twenty-Three

Cache
Be Careful - Cardi B

Morning came sooner than expected. Last night was definitely a sleepless night especially when Tony crept out with no return. At first, I thought he was just getting up to go to the bathroom or something. Maybe to even get a glass of water, but that glass of water turned into him going to the Mississippi River. This nigga has let the sun beat him home and he still had not walked through the door as of yet and it just turned 8:00 AM. I also called several times last night and it is not like him to not pick up the phone when I call. What the fuck is really happening? All I know is that nigga better be dead. If not, he just committed suicide because he had me fucked all the way up if he thought this shit was cool and that I'll be ok with it. He had my muthafuckin ass heated. My hormones were also in overdrive and I know that played a big part in my emotions. My estrogen was fully ragging. For now, though, fuck all that because Tony's ass is the perfect muthafucka to pen all my frustrations on.

Now don't get me wrong, I know I was really heated from having to be out here stuck in no man's land but that is some shit I would rather not address. It was mainly my muthfucking actions that got us down here in this God-forsaken place from jump. Of course, a bitch would never say that shit aloud. For one this isn't the time for AA meetings. Admitting to my wrongdoings is not the first step I was ready to confess to.

Once again, I have committed a hideous crime on a no-good-ass man. From the outside, muthafuckas would label me a lunatic thinking I have a problem with men. I do, but I just don't purposely go around hurting people. I didn't give them anything that they did not deserve. And if Tony knows what the fuck I know, he better have a good ass excuse for staying out all night long. Especially with his ass trying to keep the fact that we are broke from me. I already knew that shit but if he didn't have his head to far up his ass, he would know I'm not a stupid bitch. Honestly that was the least of my concerns because if Ann hadn't taught me anything in this world, she taught me the game inside and out and that is all a bitch needed to survive.

As I continued to pace across the floor, I checked the time once again becoming even more impatient with Tony as the seconds ticked by. What the fuck? I thought. Only five minutes after the hour? It felt like a lot of time had passed since the last time I checked my watch. I needed to keep myself busy or I would become a case basket at any minute.

With nothing else to do but drive myself crazy, I knew exactly that needed to be done. Really, something I should have done months ago. I went inside the master bedroom into the walk-in closet. I headed straight for the shoebox at the bottom of the stack. Even though a bitch is on the run I still made time to be fly. I lifted the top and there lie inside were a pair of shoes that had never been worn.

When I was incarcerated for those five years before getting early released on a fifteen-year sentence, I learned a few tricks that will stick with me for the rest of my life. How to become even better at getting away with things. Being locked up with all that time to just think about all the mistakes you have made and how you could have done this or that differently. That time only taught me how to be more calculated with every move I decide to make.

In this case, things were no different. In a secret department I built inside the shoes and box held a few important things and one of those things was a throwaway cell phone. Tony did not know anything about my stash and if he did, I know he would be against it. But against it or not at the end of the day he knows that I am my own woman. He also knew that there would not be anything in this world but my kids that could stop me from doing what I want. My kids are also the only reason I would go against the grain. In this situation, things are no different. Taking the chance of calling home could mean I could get caught but my hands are tied. We are broke and making sure my kids eat is more important than me and Tony's freedom.

If it wasn't for me being pregnant, I wouldn't be left stuck out to dry, but I couldn't make certain moves. Hustle is my game, but being pregnant I couldn't put in any work which is reason enough that that bitch Maya is still breathing. But only on borrowed time. As soon as I drop the load it's back to hunting season.

By 9:45 I heard Knasir getting up and moving around. I quickly put the shoes back in the box once I got what I needed out placing the box back where it was. I went to the kitchen to whip up something to eat for my baby before we both started our day. Today will be different from our usual outing. I normally will take him to tour different tourist sites just so that it will not seem that he was on lockdown just because we are fugitives. He did not ask for this shit, so I tried my best to make things as customary as possible.

Once I served the both of us and dressed, we headed out the door. There is a park down the road that I would sometimes take Knasir to when I wanted to do something as simple as clear my mind.

"Mom," my son called me in his sweet little voice as he always does.

"Yeah, big man?" I gave him my full attention.

"Can I go on the swings? I promise to be careful," he pleaded knowing I'm always on him about being careful.

"Yeah, go ahead," I said, wincing in pain.

"Are you alright momma?" Knasir grabbed my hand with concern etched across his young face.

"I'm ok. Go play baby." I told him as I took a seat on the park bench holding my stomach at the bottom. I'm out here stressing about all the shit that has happened over the last few months and Tony stupid ass adding stress on top of the rest of all this bullshit is not making it any better, I thought to myself taking the throw away phone out of my purse to make a call.

As I dialed each number slowly, I prayed that I was making the right decision. Send. I listened to the ring tone as I waited for the call to be connected.

"Hello?" I heard the familiar voice say through the phone, "Hello?" he said a little more aggressively than before. Tears came to my eyes because I missed them so much, but I realized that if I didn't speak up the phone would soon be disconnected.

"Klimax," I said in a tiny voice.

"Cache! Bitch, is that you?" I heard so much excitement in his voice. I kept quiet but not because I didn't want to talk. I was excited and was in my glory as if hearing him was too good to be true. "Bitch don't act like the cat got your tongue," he said with what I could tell was a smile on his face.

"Yeah, it is me bitch." I smiled back. "Listen though. Do you have another phone you can call me off?"

"What you mean?"

"Any other phone than yours, the one that you are on."

"Yeah, bitch I'm dialing you now so click over," Klimax said. I did.

"Bitch, where the hell have you been?"

"Around." I smiled "You know I would rather not say my location, especially on the phone. I also don't want you to have to lie for me."

"You know I will never do that Ms. Double O'Seven."

"I know, but I don't want to put you in an uncomfortable situation."

"I feel that, but I know that you ain't call me just to say what is and what isn't appropriate for me to know."

"You know me so well," I smiled. "In a few days, you will get a brochure. It will tell you everything you need, my love." With that said I hung up without even giving him time to ask any questions. On top of that, I had been watching the time as we spoke. I didn't want the call to exceed five minutes.

"Knasir. Let's go!" I yelled ready to move on to part two of my plan.

Yolanda Moore

Chapter Twenty-Four

Maya
Emotional Rollercoaster - Vivian Green

As I stood on the patio in my long champagne-colored silk robe letting the wind blow through my hair, I thought about how I have enjoyed the good life. Being here I hadn't had to suck dick or stick a nigga up to live comfortably. All Emilio, my grandfather wanted me to do is sit pretty as he prepared me for his thrown. That's exactly what I planned to do especially if it would prime me to becoming the queen I was born to be. Being a boss had to run in your blood it had to be a part of your heritage and the fact that my mother played her part and that my grandfather owned his shit muthafuckas should have already known what I was destined to be. No matter how the cut goes, fate is and always will be fate no matter how you tried to intervene in God's plan.

"Maya," Emilio's voice brought me out of my thoughts. I turned to give him my complete attention. Like I said he is a boss and when he spoke, he commanded everything to cease.

"Yes?" I answered.

"We have an emergency. Margaret has been carried to the hospital and the baby will be born pretty soon. I won't be there, but I think it is best that you go off and celebrate the life of this child being born." I didn't need to speak, I just nodded in response because I was really too afraid of what would really come out. What I wanted to say was, "If you aren't going, what makes you think I would want to be there?" But I didn't. I kept that shit to myself as he walked off knowing when he spoke there wasn't anything else left to say.

*****

By the time I dressed and made it to the hospital, Margerret was still in labor. I don't know who her ass had decided to go out and get knocked up by. However, no one was here but me and if I was honest with myself it wasn't because that is what my heart desired.

For the baby's sake, I tried plastering a smile on my face and pretended to be passionate about the creation that is being birthed. On some real shit though, I really did feel sorry for her. Why? Because I knew how it felt not to have anyone to be there to support you. I know how bad that shit hurt, and I know that familiar feeling of being alone.

Damn. Not even her own father wanted to be here for her. I don't know what could have gone wrong with them that Emilio could not even put his ill feelings aside for the birth of his first grandson. But then again that is the life of the "filthy rich" for your ass. I thought, shaking my head as I imagined what it would be like once I got my paws on the type of money Emilio is holding. Hopefully I won't be as cruel as he is when it comes to blood.

"Ma'am, could you please sanitize? We are about to deliver a healthy baby boy. Here is the proper PPE you will need in order to move forward labor," a fine ass doctor with a thick ass accent said, smiling and walking off after handing me the PPE.

After I got dressed, I headed toward the door of the delivery room. My heart skipped several beats. Fuck, I did not know what to expect. I never did any shit like this and still wasn't certain if I was ready now. Right when I reached the door, I took a deep breath. Inhale. Exhale. And then I stepped inside ready to get this shit over with.

*****

Cache

After leaving the post office all that was left for me to do was wait. I wrote to Klimax on the brochure explaining everything that needed to be done. I could have done that in the first place but knowing him I knew he wasn't just going to fall for that shit unless he heard it from the horse's mouth.

The first thought Klimax would have had was that someone was fucking with him and trying to set him up. So, me taking the chance by calling was very necessary.

It was now approaching two o'clock p.m. and I needed to get home to wait on Tony. I was straight busting him in his shit yeah, I'm pregnant but my hand or his face isn't.

I called yet another Uber to take us home. I know Knasir would not be ready to head in, but the sky had become cloudy and I didn't want to be caught in the change of climate.

When the Uber pulled up to pick us up, I felt another sharp pain at the bottom of my stomach. I shook it off not thinking it too serious. The pain reminded me of having my cycle so I knew it couldn't have meant anything bad.

On our ride back home, the sky began to cry and so did I, silently. The view took me back to a time that I will never forget. The day A'nett was buried. Damn. Being pregnant really is sending me on a wild emotional roller coaster ride and I couldn't wait to push her out. It is a miracle that she has survived with all the stress I have been under lately. *She's a miracle*, I thought. Antonio? A'nett? Amiracle. That's exactly what I will name her. If I'm really having a girl. I haven't been to any checkups since we've been on the run, but I have been taking prenatal vitamins only because they are sold over the counter. Really wasn't sure how many months I am. I should only be about six which is why I don't understand the cramps. Hopefully, I wasn't going through what I went through with my little man. I had him premature at seven months and I hope that isn't the case this time, I thought rubbing my belly. So, I should have at least three more months until she drops.

Finally, we pulled up to the house and by the time we did it was raining cats and dogs. I could barely see what's in front of me. Honestly, I couldn't tell if my vision was blurry and playing tricks on me from the dizziness I had begun to feel or if it was from the catastrophe going on outside the Uber. When I looked out in the direction of what had become our home, I could see two silhouettes standing as if they were waiting on our arrival.

Coming to a complete stop, I proceeded to get out of the car despite how I felt after paying for my fare. All I wanted was my bed, but I also wanted to know who the fuck is on my porch? I know it wasn't Tony and I prayed it wasn't the authorities coming to arrest me.

"Come on ma! Look at grams and pops!" My baby yelled jumping out of the car headfirst into the rain before I could tell him to chill.

Grams and pops, I thought with a look of confusion on my face. I got out of the car still wondering how they knew where we were. Why are they here? I took note as everything around me started to move slow. As soon as my feet touched the pavement, another cramp hit me. This time there was a warm liquid flowing down my legs. Damn, am I that delusional that I pissed myself? Looking down, I was shocked to see a crimson color that faded to a light pink as the rain washed away the evidence of blood.

I reacted by flabbergasting, sending my heart into a convulsion. "What the fuck is goin' on?" I asked myself. "Calm down," I tried coaxing myself to remain repose, but with all the fucking blood that shit just wasn't happening.

When I looked back up Grams and Pops were running toward me in a hurry. Before they could reach me though, that is when everything surrounding me disappeared.

142

Chapter Twenty-Five

Klimax
Explode - Big Freeda

I've been waiting for two damn days to see when in the fuck I was going to hear from Cache. All I know is that I was supposed to be waiting for a damn brochure. Until finally it came in the mail. Playing the waiting game had me on edge like a muthafucka and now I could breathe since the day has arrived.

Now for the most challenging. Getting Chanel ass on board. Not that she didn't love her sister because she did. The thing is her sass gone be fifty shades of burnt the fuck up because Cache decided to contact me instead of her. She isn't going to see the logic in Cache's reason.

Cache knows that it would be less likely for the boys in blue to still be watching me and not Chanel. I know when all that shit Cache got herself caught up in like a whore caught in fishnets, they were on Chanel back like a backpack. So, if my bestie wanted to be mad so be it! I would rather her be mad than our sister being caught.

"Baby," I said softly knocking on Richard's office door before I opened it to enter.

"Yeah?" he said. "Come in." I know how busy he could be when he was at work and I also knew he could be a totally different person when he was behind these doors. I walked in sexually to give him something to smile about just in case he is in one of his stressful moods.

I walked up to him wrapping my arms around his neck kissing his earlobe. "Why are you so stressed, babe?" I asked as I started to rub his shoulders.

"It's just work. Nothing to worry your pretty little head over," he said as he still gave all of his attention to his computer screen.

Oh really? I raised my right eyebrow. I'ma show him how pretty my little head is I continued with my thoughts as I crawled under his desk unzipping his trousers.

I wrapped my slim fingers around his shaft as if his shit was the mic and I was ready to vocalize. I wet my tongue just like he liked and ran my tongue clean across the tip tasting the pre-cum that glistened right on the head.

"Mmmu," I moan, receiving more pleasure than he was. I sucked his dick for a pastime as if I was watching my favorite lifetime movie.

"Shittt, why you do this to me?" Richard also moaned,. He loved the feeling of my throat and how I made it contract. I could usually have his ass cum in less than five minutes but that only happens when I play in his back door. Not today though buddy, I thought as I continued to work my hand, mouth, and tongue at the same damn time.

I instantly felt his leg stiff up and that told the story, and I knew I was doing my muthafucking job. Still sucking his dick without missing a beat as I pushed the chair back, we both knew what time it was. In one swift motion, we switched positions and I promise you that dick did not fall from my mouth.

He was now in a standing position holding my weave for dear life as he fucked my face just the way I liked it. What could I say? I was blessed to not have a gag reflex, so I took that shit like a G as he KO'd my face. Once his balls started slapping my chin, I already knew it was time to swallow his children. Trust me when I say I didn't have a problem with ingesting that shit either because I swear I didn't need any more of his fucking children running around this bitch getting any of what belonged to me.

As he came in my mouth, I drank that shit like water with a smile on my face, because what I didn't want to do I knew the next bitch wouldn't mind. That is what required fucking with a man like Richard. He had so much fucking money if he asked my ass to fuck a horse best believe it's going down in this muthafucka. I would just have to find the best doctors to reconstruct my ass hole.

"Thanks, bae," he said as I got off my knees with pride. I know my grandfather is rolling around in his grave with the way I bowed down to suck a white man's cock voluntarily.

But a girl's gotta do what a girl gotta do, I wiped my mouth.

"Babe, I need a fav?" I said in my whiney voice.

"What is it? Anything babe. Just name it." And see? That is exactly why I didn't mind sucking this man dick whenever, wherever. My last nigga was a straight nigga in every sense of the word. After I got his ass off, he would beat my ass leaving me crying with a busted eye and a bloody mouth that just sucked his dick. His reason? Because my head was good enough to get my ass beat. It was also a reminder to think twice before I thought of giving *his* shit away as if he had just sucked his own dick. Negro, please! I got the fuck on down away from his ass, but not because he beat me. The sad part is I would have stayed, ass whooping's and all. That was until I found that nigga letting a bitch suck the same dick that caused me to get boxed up.

"Is it money that you need?" Richard asked, bringing me out of my past life.

"No baby I have enough of that. You always bless me with no rainy days," I thought about the account he has set up for me just in case something happened to him.

"Well, what is it?" he asked. "Is it anything about the wedding plans?" he asked. *Fuck no!* I thought. *The only thing I'm worried about is that is for the damn divorce to be finalized.*

"No baby, we have that under control. Don't we?" Not giving him time to respond I continued. "I just want a little time off so that I can go on a vacay with my girlfriend, Chanel, that is all." I looked up at him giving him my sexiest look.

"Well, that isn't a problem. I have told you several times that you don't even have to come to the office. Take as many trips as you want?" he smiled bending down to kiss me. *Muthafucka, please!* I thought smiling once we pulled apart. Like I said he is a walking bank and I needed to keep my eyes on him especially at the office. I would hate to have to beat a muthafucka down in that bitch. I remembered the times I would meet Richard at the office to suck his dick before he and his ex-wife split. So, no sir, not gonna happen.

"Thanks, my love. You know I love working at the office though, that isn't a problem. Plus, I like being around when you're stressed," I said, grabbing his butt cheeks to bring him in for another kiss.

*****

In less than forty-five minutes I was out the door rushing over to Chanel's crib. I still haven't put my plan together of how I should come at her. Should I tell her the truth? If I did it would be a never-ending argument. But if I just told her we were going on a girl's trip. I will not get any lip at all. "You know what?" I asked myself I will give her the real once we board the plane. That way her ass won't be able to storm off because we would both already be down there," I said aloud as I made plans to fly out tonight.

Cache had also booked flights for the both of us and also asked for me to bring a couple of racks with me. That will not be a problem because my man had money out the ass. Cache and Chanel have money too especially after the loss of their brother, Carnel.

That shit was a crying shame the way he was left out in the streets but at least he left his sisters set for life. Right? Anyway, as I was saying, good thing that I have the money to give because if I didn't I would have to kill Chanel for being so damn stubborn once she found out Cache contacted me.

As soon as I pulled up in front of Exclusive Hair salon I hopped out of my car and walked into the place as if I owned that mutha.

"Hello, ladies?" I spoke as my heels clicked across the floor as I walked to the back making sure to put an extra twist in my walk. Beauty shop gossip always turned into a horror movie. Don't let a bitch catch you walking with your head down because them bitches will concoct a whole muthafucking story as if it came straight out of the horse's mouth itself. These bitches here are some storytelling ass hoes. I bet they could write a story just as legendary as my girl Adrienne who wrote: "When A Good Girl Goes Bad." Now that is some shit you cannot just make up. A bitch had to live that shit go through it and concur it in order to tell a saga so great.

"Chanel, darling?" I smiled as I walked through her office door. Instead of her meeting me with her usual beautiful smile, she was blank-faced and stuck behind a damn desk. This time I won't be crawling under to relieve any stress.

"Yes, how can I help you?" she asked, looking over her glasses..

"Ah fuck no! Really bitch? I know damn well you not giving me the *how can I help you* bullshit. I know exactly what you need my love?" I said walking around to pull her from her seat.

"Damn bitch and what is that?" she asked, sounding disinterested in what I had to say but I knew exactly what to do to make this bitch smile, I pulled the two flight tickets for a round trip to Mexico. "These bad bitches right here are complimentary of my man... your brother-in-law, Richard." When she still had not busted a smile, I knew I had to go even harder for this bitch to fold.

She gave a hard bargain, but trust me, she isn't my bestie for nothing. "Alright hoe you gon' do a bitch like that? I'ma throw a damn shopping spree with it." I tossed my hand on my hip which brought a smile to her face.

"Let's go bitch!" She grabbed me by the hand, dragging me out of the shop.

Chapter Twenty-Six

Tony
I Got You - Kevin Gates

Damn. Last night I fell asleep in the bed with D'zyna. not that anything happened. She did try to suck, fuck, and duck a nigga, but that shit is for the birds. There is only one thing on my mind and that was finding a way to Emilio and have a seat with him at the round table. Considering that I pushed dope for him I knew the muthafucka would at least hear a nigga out.

I dressed quickly using the bathroom to shower and the hotel toothbrush to hit my grill before I bounced. I quietly stepped out of the bathroom doing my best to not wake D'zyna. As I walked over to the table, I grabbed my shit I could see her out my peripheral as she tossed in her sleep. I kept doing what I was doing as if I didn't see her.

"So, you really gonna just walk out the door without telling me goodbye at least?" she asked still with sleep in her voice.

"Nah shawty I'm just doing what I would if you weren't here. No hard feelings." I continued with what I was doing.

"Tony? At least promise me you will contact me to let me know that you are ok? Last night we might not have crossed that line but daddy I promise I could feel the way you fucked me without even looking at me."

"Look ma," I said turning to her giving her my full attention. "I got a family and I love them. That's why I'm out here robbing muthafuckas and shit to make sure me and mine are straight. But if we were living in another life, I promise you it would be on and popping. But it's not in this lifetime," I told her as I checked the clip in my gun before tucking it back in my waistband of my pant.

"Alright, that is fine. I have never been a desperate bitch and I don't want to sound like one now," she said as she stood in only her bra and panties looking right. I promise I didn't touch her, but it was definitely hard not to fuck. I am still a man. Just not a dog ass nigga. "This time though," she said walking up to me wrapping her arms around my neck. "I'ma save face. If things don't work out with the two of you, look a bitch up. I know a real one when I see one. I'm the only bitch on Facebook name D'zyna. Type it in and you'll find me. I promise," she said kissing my lips and I let her tongue and all. Cache would bury my ass for this bullshit. Good thing I will never see this chick again because I don't know how strong I could be if we crossed paths again.

*****

Cache

Damn. What the fuck happened to me? I was no longer soaking in the rain, but in the comfort of a bed, I thought opening my eyes. All I remember was blood everywhere, my in-laws, and then everything around me going black. Now here I am opening my eyes in a damn hospital. Hospital! I started to hyperventilate. *Did something happen to my baby? My baby, oh my God not my baby!* My hands flew to my stomach. My soul felt disconnected. "What happened to my baby?" I cried.

When I realized my baby was missing, I started snatching I.V.'s from my arms but as I went to swing my legs across the bed, they were dead. Senseless. Unconscious. Up until now, I didn't notice that I couldn't feel my fucking legs. Am I paralyzed? What in the hell happened to me while I was out of it? Where is everyone? Knasir.

"Nurse! Nurse!" I shouted to get someone's attention. Within a few minutes, two nurses came running to my rescue.

"Are you alright?" one of them asked me with a look of concern on her face as the other one looked all ugly and shit. Or was it a natural look? Bitch!

"Noooo. I'm not! Where is my baby?" I whined from the lack of understanding.

"Ma'am! Ma'am just stay calm…"

"Stay calm!" I shouted back, cutting that bitches ass off like k-camp.

"How the fuck am I supposed to do that? I'm up in this bitch for God only knows what and I wake the fuck up blindsided with no fucking baby that I came in this bitch carrying in my damn stomach. Now she saying look for me and you." I pointed looking her dead in her eyes. "Give me a fucking reason to stay calm because ever since I opened my eyes, I haven't had one as of fucking yet." Before anyone of the nurses could respond in ran my baby boy. Thank God!

"Momma. Momma. We have our baby and she wants to meet you." My son's voice is like music to my ears. Boy was I glad to see him. His grandparents came walking in right behind him with the biggest smile on their faces In Gram's arms was my little bundle of joy. It seemed like it is taking forever for them to get to me and the anticipation is killing me. I felt like I'm at a gender reveal.

The nurses that I had just almost committed murder on were still standing there, but now smiling even after the show I put on. I mean what did they expect? I'm a concerned mother at the end of the day and in order for them to still be standing there smiling after the way I acted out they must have been mothers as well.

However, not a soul in this world meant more than the two-little people in her. I am definitely basking in glory and nothing could take that away from me. Not even Tony muthafucking ass for not being here. I must admit though I am still a little salty with the nigga and I can't lie I'ma fuck his ass up.

"What are you going to name her momma?" Never looking up from her pretty face. Even though most people who would look at her might not see she looked just like her father.

"A'miracle."

*****

Tony

"Fuck!" I slammed my hand on the steering wheel. I just left the house and Cache or Knasir isn't there. I was speeding on my way to the nearest hospital. Something had to be going on with the baby. When I made it home, the first thing I noticed was blood all over the front porch. Something just wasn't right. I did go inside the house to check every room to make sure that they both were not inside hurt.

At that moment I did not know what to expect. That was until I ran across a piece of stationary paper that had a note scribbled across. It wasn't Cache's handwriting so that really made me angry with myself that another muthafucka had been here for her and I kicked myself in the ass for not being where I should have been. All in all, I had to admit I had to count my blessings because at least someone had been here to assist her. I just pray that God could extend that blessing a little more and protect my family. I don't know what the fuck I would do if something happened to them.

"Fuck, I should've been here!" I said aloud to myself. The only thing that is going to stop Cache from killing my ass is the fact that we will be able to go back home.

After conversing with Emilio, he told me he would be able to help me in more ways than one. All he had to do was make a call and make shit happen. He used one of his favors at the D.A.'s office and got someone to cop to the murder charges for Cache and me. Although no one knew besides Cache and Emilio that I had killed that nurse back in Baton Rouge. I didn't need that shit coming back later to bite me in the ass. So, if you ask me, I killed two birds with one stone.

Just as I was headed on to tell Cache the good news, I am slapped in the face with what I hope isn't a tragedy.

When I pulled up to the hospital's entrance, I parked in the fire zone, but I didn't give a fuck. I had my mind on one thing and one thing only.

I ran straight for the front desk. I stood there for a second trying to be as patient as possible with the receptionist but this muthafucka found more interest in her fucking phone call. The fucked-up thing is her ass sees me standing here and still won't make eye contact with me. You know what? Fuck it.

"Listen bitch I tried being patient with you, but my fucking wife has come in here with my son and pregnant with my other child. If you knew what the fuck I know, you would be trying to assist me not now but right NOW!" I looked at her with the look of the devil in my eyes as I hung up the phone.

She looked at me as if she was appalled but she might as well pick up her fucking lip. I don't like disrespecting women, but this hoe has pushed my damn buttons.

"Damn, what is her name?" She asked with anger. This Spanish bitch had an attitude like a sistah.

Once I gave her Cache's name, she typed it in the system giving her room number. When I received her room number, I shot out toward her direction. As soon as I curved around the door frame, my eyes misted over upon seeing my family.

"Could everyone excuse us?" Cache asked when we locked eyes. On her face, you couldn't see anger but when I looked into her soul, I knew what I was in for. I slightly prayed that everyone in the room saw what I saw and objected to her request. Most niggas back at home feared me and I walked this earth without a care in the world but when it came to Cache Price, I can't lie bae brought me to my knees.

Without anyone saying anything, they did what was asked because just like I knew Cache they did too.

"Momma, what about me? Can I stay?" Knasir asked, still sitting upon the bed on the side of Cache and our baby girl.

"No big man I need to talk to Tony but if you would go with Grams and Pops to go get us a snack, I would appreciate it." she kissed the top of his head, and just like a momma's boy he did what was asked and the room was cleared out just like that. FUCK.

"Tell me what's up Tony or we can just go straight to til death do us part? Bitch because if I feel you playing with me, I'ma send yo ass back home zipped up," she spat with so much aggression as soon as the door closed.

"Listen ma, I promise you. I was out making shit happen for us.

"Fuck you mean? The only thing I would appreciate you making happen is to get us out of this fucking hole we are falling in. I know we're broke and before you deny the shit think about who the fuck I am, Tony." I held my head down for the first time during our relationship.

"Look ma you know I would lay my life down for the three of you. I would never lie to you I just didn't want you under so much pressure with the baby and shit Cache that's all." I picked my head up looking her in the eyes as I grabbed her hand. "Bae I'm sorry but like I said I would go whatever it takes to protect you, us, and our kids." I pleaded for the hundredth time and if I had to a hundred more I would. "Speaking of protecting and all that good shit. I got good news for you?"

"What is it Tony?" she asked I could tell from the look in her eyes that I was getting through to her. "I'm listening."

"We can finally go home," I smiled at her waiting on her reaction.

"What? What you just said? Don't fuck with me Tony?" she said thinking I was bullshitting her

"Na baby girl I'll never fuck with ya head like that. We are getting the fuck from here and going back to Baton Rouge We cleared of all them charges my love."

"How?" she asked

"It doesn't even matter my love. Just know I do what needs to be done for me and mine," I said keeping it simple. What I didn't want to tell her is how I sold my soul to the devil.

Yolanda Moore

Chapter Twenty-Seven

Chanel
OTW - DJ Luke Nasty

"Bitch I could really kick your fucking ass right now! I can't believe you lied and acted like we were going on a girl's trip. You can't be trusted hoe that shit is fucked up!" I whined. Honestly, I was burnt up because my own damned sister didn't think to call me. I'm the bitch she has been knowing all her fucking life. I would have thought if anything she'd call me before anyone on this earth.

"Chanel really? That isn't fair, don't be mad at me honey honey." Klimax had the nerve to try and hug my arm. I jerked it back.

"Life isn't fair," I said as we walked over to baggage claim.

"What could I do to make it up to you?"

"I don't know but we can start off first with a shopping spree."

"Alright let's go now!" Klimax said always looking for an opportunity to go shopping.

"Well, we gon' find this fucking sister of mine first, then after I kick her ass, we are going blow Richard's ass off the map," I said as we got an Uber. Right before we hopped in the car, I swear I could feel someone watching. I just shook it off. I know I was still fucked up with that officer getting knocked off in front me. Finally. We booked a room. It took us forever to even find a room available, but I should have known Klimax's ass. Whenever Klimax did some sneaky shit something always went wrong. Klimax knows we are like PB&J so wherever he fucked up I had his back. This time is no different. Not wasting any more time or energy on that thought I quickly washed my juice box and hopped my ass straight in the bed without passing go or collecting two hundred dollars. A bitch was tired, and I didn't have any fight left in me. Tomorrow though is a whole other day and hopefully I will be putting my size seven in my sister's ass.

*****

Klimax

Chanel took this trip better than what I thought she would, I thought as I got ready for bed. I know the only reason she kept as calm as she was is because she knew that shopping spree I agreed to will come at a big price. I wasn't tripping at all because when your man is *the man*, the racks I'ma be spending, after all, will be nothing. Richard won't even miss the money we were surely going to blow.

Speaking of Richard, I needed to call him to check in. I didn't want him worried sick about me, I thought as I dialed his number. I waited as his phone rang. Usually, it didn't take him long to pick up when I called. Maybe he had fallen asleep or something, so I hung up. I didn't want to seem too pressed. Fucking with a man like Richard, you still have to portray as if you didn't need his ass especially when you suck him off leaving his ass speechless. You make that nigga miss you even when you stuck on stupid behind his ass give him his space.

All I know is his ass better be sleep by his muthafucking self or I was gone hit his ass with that pressure if he played on my top.

At the moment though shit isn't about me and Richard, I thought as I closed my eyes excited about seeing Cache even if it would break my heart to have to leave her once again.

The next morning came sooner than expected and even though I could use a few more hours of beauty rest I knew I had shit to do. First things first I tried calling the number that Cache called me from just to let her know that we were here, and I would be meeting her at the appointed time.

She didn't answer but I just assumed because it was still early. 7:08 AM to be exact I didn't have to meet her until 10:00 AM, but still.

"Fuck it, let me just shower first." When I got in the shower, I couldn't help myself. I began to cry. I had been keeping a secret from everyone including Chanel. I knew if I couldn't tell her what weighed heavily on my heart, I couldn't tell anyone. So, with that thought I cried, this shit had been weighing on my heart like a muthafucka. I used everything going on good in my life as a distraction. That is how unbearable this shit is which is one reason I was excited and desperate to hear from Cache. In due time though it will all be over.

I had to keep telling myself I was doing the right thing. Then on the flip side, I could have just given Chanel all the info and let her come through for her sister instead of me. How selfish of me though?

At last, I got out of the shower. I towel dried myself as my stomach became hollow. Just a few days ago, I wasn't feeling this way when Cache called. But I guess since the day is finally here, my feelings have changed.

After getting dressed, I checked my phone for missed calls and just as expected there were several that I missed. Trust me when I say I wasn't looking forward to them. I guess the calls were meant to be a reminder of what I committed myself to.

"Alright. Get it together girl you can do this," I talked myself into what was about to happen. *All I had to do is meet Cache and drop off the money,* I thought.

"Come on now, hoe. I've been waiting on you to get dressed. What's taking you so damned long?" Chanel asked, coming through the door that connected our rooms.

"Bitch, I been up since 7:00 waiting on your ass," I told her not wanting to expose the fact that I couldn't sleep and trust I had a reason.

"Well, hoe it's 9:15 now so let's get this shit started because I should've given her ass a long time ago."

"Alright. Let me call her to let her know I'm on my way."

"Hello?" I heard a voice come through the phone that wasn't Cache's voice.

"Can I speak to Cache please?"

"Yeah, sure could you hold?" Before I could tell them that I didn't mind holding the phone was being exchanged from one hand to another.

"Hello?" I heard Cache say through the phone as if she had just woken up.

"This me bitch Klimax what's really going on? I thought I was meeting you this morning. I know damn well you didn't forget your ass called me way down here?"

"Shit. I'm sorry I actually did. Yesterday has been rough for me and the day before that I was hospitalized."

"Hospitalized?"

"Yeah. Look take this address down. It's for the hospital I'll explain once you get here. Oh, and tell my sister I love her even though I know she is mad."

"Bitch whatever just know I want my one when we get up there," Chanel yelled over my shoulder before I could deliver the message.

After taking the address down I disconnected the call then quickly sent a text message because of the change of plans.

"Damn bitch, what? Did Richard's old ass make you downgrade on your phone?" Chanel said, taking notice of the burner I had.

"Bitch please, you should know I'll never downgrade when it comes to Richard. My phone is broken, that's all. Just waiting on my new phone to come through," I said hoping she would stop questioning me about my damn phone. "Anyway, let's go see your damn sister because her ass is just full of surprises," I said changing the subject just as quickly as it had come.

Yolanda Moore

C.R.E.A.M. 2

Chapter Twenty-Eight

Cache
Devils - Boosie Bad Azz

"Bae, who was that?" Tony asked me with a look of curiosity on his face.

"Klimax and Chanel. You should know just like you, I will always have my ways of taking care of this family also," I said, needing to explain myself.

"So, you were willing to take the chance of us getting popped?" he asked me.

"Fucking right you were willing to take the chance of my kids out kids losing their father. Sometimes we do stupid shit for the ones we love but trust me when I say my shit was legitimate but now that you say we clean we good right? No more hiding?" I asked, taking his hand.

"Yeah ma. We are good. Tomorrow you will be released and when you do, we'll be heading home to start our forever."

Just when Tony finished his sentence, I heard someone coming through the door. I looked up expecting it to be Chanel and Klimax, but to my surprise, two detectives walked in instead. Without them even having to introduce themselves, I knew what it was hitting for.

"My name is Detective Tate, may I come in?" My fucking heart hit the floor.

"Fuck you asking for if you are already stepping inside the room?" Tony said before I could say anything. He seemed like his cool, calm, and collected self. What he said about the charges being dropped had to be true because they'd be on our ass like white on rice. Being that they came in here as if they had the common sense the Lord gave them, it must be true. And still, at the moment, we are not being read our rights.

"Antonio Clark, I really think it's in your best interest that you shut the fuck up if I were you." A second detective walked through the door making sure his gun was visual. With my hand still on Tony's, I squeezed it letting him know to chill out. Our baby is more important than these muthafuckas having a pissing contest or seeing who has the biggest dick. *This shit isn't about that*, I thought hoping he could read my mind at the fucking moment. When he did not say shit back, I knew right then and there, there must truly be a God. I knew Tony. His head could sometimes be bigger than his dick and he hated letting shit slide.

"How can I help you, officer?" I decided to speak up because someone in the room needs to be an adult.

"We need to question the both of you about a murder. You and Antonio will be going back with us across the border." Detective Tate spoke up again.

"We are no longer wanted for murder officer the charges have been dropped. And besides, the person that committed that crime has been arrested. So why would we be answering any of your questions? With all due respect," I added, letting him know I knew the deal.

"What about jurisdiction does that count?" asked Tony.

"No, no, no," the detective said smiling. "You don't get to play the game and make the rules," he was saying when I spotted Chanel bending the doorframe.

"What the fuck is going on in here?" she asked with a look of surprise on her face. She never broke eye contact with the detective. Klimax was right on her heels not saying a word.

"Ma'am, you can't come in here..."

"What you mean? This is my damn sister and brother-in-law! And the last time we were in a room together, you left someone lying in my living room dead and I have been fucked up ever since."

What the fuck is really going on? Someone dead in her living room?

"Did you fucking follow us?"

"You know what?" the detective who never introduced himself said. "I didn't come here for the bullshit. I came to arrest you and you know what? Fuck Jurisdiction. Laws are meant to be broken. You both are under arrest."

"No. No. No! Chanel come get my baby and bond me out wherever the fuck they take me." Before A'miracle was in Chanel's arms good, I was being arrested and carried out the room because at the moment I had no fucking clue what could have gone wrong. How could they have found us? Did I fuck up by calling Klimax?

The more I thought about the shit and the reason I was being detained was simple. Cash always ruled, but this time the cash I spoke of wasn't me. The saying is, be careful what you ask for because you just might get it. I just pray that this isn't part of starting our forever like Tony promised.

To Be Continued...

C.R.E.A.M. 3
Coming Soon

Submission Guideline

Submit the first three chapters of your completed manuscript to ldpsubmissions@gmail.com, subject line: Your book's title. The manuscript must be in a .doc file and sent as an attachment. Document should be in Times New Roman, double spaced and in size 12 font. Also, provide your synopsis and full contact information. If sending multiple submissions, they must each be in a separate email.

Have a story but no way to send it electronically? You can still submit to LDP/Ca$h Presents. Send in the first three chapters, written or typed, of your completed manuscript to:

LDP: Submissions Dept
Po Box 944
Stockbridge, Ga 30281

DO NOT send original manuscript. Must be a duplicate.

Provide your synopsis and a cover letter containing your full contact information.

Thanks for considering LDP and Ca$h Presents.

C.R.E.A.M. 2

By **Ghost**

A HUSTLER'S DECEIT III

KILL ZONE **II**

BAE BELONGS TO ME III

A DOPE BOY'S QUEEN III

By **Aryanna**

COKE KINGS V

KING OF THE TRAP III

By **T.J. Edwards**

GORILLAZ IN THE BAY V

3X KRAZY III

De'Kari

THE STREETS ARE CALLING II

Duquie Wilson

KINGPIN KILLAZ IV

STREET KINGS III

PAID IN BLOOD III

CARTEL KILLAZ IV

DOPE GODS III

Hood Rich

SINS OF A HUSTLA II

ASAD

KINGZ OF THE GAME VI

Playa Ray

SLAUGHTER GANG IV

RUTHLESS HEART IV

C.R.E.A.M. 2

By Willie Slaughter

FUK SHYT II

By Blakk Diamond

TRAP QUEEN

By Troublesome

YAYO V

GHOST MOB II

Stilloan Robinson

KINGPIN DREAMS III

By Paper Boi Rari

CREAM III

By Yolanda Moore

SON OF A DOPE FIEND III

HEAVEN GOT A GHETTO II

By Renta

FOREVER GANGSTA II

GLOCKS ON SATIN SHEETS III

By Adrian Dulan

LOYALTY AIN'T PROMISED III

By Keith Williams

THE PRICE YOU PAY FOR LOVE III

By Destiny Skai

I'M NOTHING WITHOUT HIS LOVE II

SINS OF A THUG II

By Monet Dragun

LIFE OF A SAVAGE IV

Yolanda Moore

MURDA SEASON IV

GANGLAND CARTEL IV

CHI'RAQ GANGSTAS IV

KILLERS ON ELM STREET II

JACK BOYZ N DA BRONX II

By **Romell Tukes**

QUIET MONEY IV

EXTENDED CLIP III

THUG LIFE IV

By **Trai'Quan**

THE STREETS MADE ME III

By **Larry D. Wright**

IF YOU CROSS ME ONCE II

ANGEL III

By **Anthony Fields**

FRIEND OR FOE III

By **Mimi**

SAVAGE STORMS III

By **Meesha**

BLOOD ON THE MONEY III

By J-Blunt

THE STREETS WILL NEVER CLOSE II

By K'ajji

NIGHTMARES OF A HUSTLA III

By King Dream

170

C.R.E.A.M. 2

IN THE ARM OF HIS BOSS

By Jamila

MONEY, MURDER & MEMORIES III

Malik D. Rice

CONCRETE KILLAZ II

By Kingpen

HARD AND RUTHLESS II

By Von Wiley Hall

LEVELS TO THIS SHYT II

By Ah'Million

MOB TIES II

By SayNoMore

BODYMORE MURDERLAND II

By Delmont Player

THE LAST OF THE OGS II

Tranay Adams

FOR THE LOVE OF A BOSS II

By C. D. Blue

Available Now

RESTRAINING ORDER **I & II**

By **CA$H & Coffee**

LOVE KNOWS NO BOUNDARIES **I II & III**

171

Yolanda Moore

By **Coffee**

RAISED AS A GOON I, II, III & IV

BRED BY THE SLUMS I, II, III

BLAST FOR ME I & II

ROTTEN TO THE CORE I II III

A BRONX TALE I, II, III

DUFFLE BAG CARTEL I II III IV V

HEARTLESS GOON I II III IV V

A SAVAGE DOPEBOY I II

DRUG LORDS I II III

CUTTHROAT MAFIA I II

By **Ghost**

LAY IT DOWN **I & II**

LAST OF A DYING BREED I II

BLOOD STAINS OF A SHOTTA I & II III

By **Jamaica**

LOYAL TO THE GAME I II III

LIFE OF SIN I, II III

By **TJ & Jelissa**

BLOODY COMMAS I & II

SKI MASK CARTEL I II & III

KING OF NEW YORK I II,III IV V

RISE TO POWER I II III

COKE KINGS I II III IV

BORN HEARTLESS I II III IV

KING OF THE TRAP I II

C.R.E.A.M. 2

By **T.J. Edwards**

IF LOVING HIM IS WRONG...I & II

LOVE ME EVEN WHEN IT HURTS I II III

By **Jelissa**

WHEN THE STREETS CLAP BACK I & II III

THE HEART OF A SAVAGE I II III

By **Jibril Williams**

A DISTINGUISHED THUG STOLE MY HEART I II & III

LOVE SHOULDN'T HURT I II III IV

RENEGADE BOYS I II III IV

PAID IN KARMA I II III

SAVAGE STORMS I II

By **Meesha**

A GANGSTER'S CODE I &, II III

A GANGSTER'S SYN I II III

THE SAVAGE LIFE I II III

CHAINED TO THE STREETS I II III

BLOOD ON THE MONEY I II

By J-Blunt

PUSH IT TO THE LIMIT

By **Bre' Hayes**

BLOOD OF A BOSS **I, II, III, IV, V**

SHADOWS OF THE GAME

TRAP BASTARD

By **Askari**

THE STREETS BLEED MURDER **I, II & III**

Yolanda Moore

THE HEART OF A GANGSTA I II& III
By **Jerry Jackson**
CUM FOR ME I II III IV V VI
An **LDP Erotica Collaboration**
BRIDE OF A HUSTLA **I II & II**
THE FETTI GIRLS **I, II& III**
CORRUPTED BY A GANGSTA I, II III, IV
BLINDED BY HIS LOVE
THE PRICE YOU PAY FOR LOVE I II
DOPE GIRL MAGIC I II III
By **Destiny Skai**
WHEN A GOOD GIRL GOES BAD
By **Adrienne**
THE COST OF LOYALTY I II III
By Kweli
A GANGSTER'S REVENGE **I II III & IV**
THE BOSS MAN'S DAUGHTERS I II III IV V
A SAVAGE LOVE **I & II**
BAE BELONGS TO ME I II
A HUSTLER'S DECEIT I, II, III
WHAT BAD BITCHES DO I, II, III
SOUL OF A MONSTER I II III
KILL ZONE
A DOPE BOY'S QUEEN I II
By **Aryanna**
A KINGPIN'S AMBITON

174

C.R.E.A.M. 2

A KINGPIN'S AMBITION **II**

I MURDER FOR THE DOUGH

By **Ambitious**

TRUE SAVAGE I II III IV V VI VII

DOPE BOY MAGIC I, II, III

MIDNIGHT CARTEL I II III

CITY OF KINGZ I II

By **Chris Green**

A DOPEBOY'S PRAYER

By **Eddie "Wolf" Lee**

THE KING CARTEL **I, II & III**

By **Frank Gresham**

THESE NIGGAS AIN'T LOYAL **I, II & III**

By **Nikki Tee**

GANGSTA SHYT **I II &III**

By **CATO**

THE ULTIMATE BETRAYAL

By **Phoenix**

BOSS'N UP **I , II & III**

By **Royal Nicole**

I LOVE YOU TO DEATH

By Destiny J

I RIDE FOR MY HITTA

I STILL RIDE FOR MY HITTA

By **Misty Holt**

LOVE & CHASIN' PAPER

Yolanda Moore

By **Qay Crockett**
TO DIE IN VAIN
SINS OF A HUSTLA
By **ASAD**
BROOKLYN HUSTLAZ
By **Boogsy Morina**
BROOKLYN ON LOCK I & II
By **Sonovia**
GANGSTA CITY
By **Teddy Duke**
A DRUG KING AND HIS DIAMOND I & II III
A DOPEMAN'S RICHES
HER MAN, MINE'S TOO I, II
CASH MONEY HO'S
THE WIFEY I USED TO BE I II
By **Nicole Goosby**
TRAPHOUSE KING **I II & III**
KINGPIN KILLAZ I II III
STREET KINGS I II
PAID IN BLOOD **I II**
CARTEL KILLAZ I II III
DOPE GODS I II
By **Hood Rich**
LIPSTICK KILLAH **I, II, III**
CRIME OF PASSION I II & III
FRIEND OR FOE I II

C.R.E.A.M. 2

By **Mimi**
STEADY MOBBN' **I, II, III**
THE STREETS STAINED MY SOUL
By **Marcellus Allen**
WHO SHOT YA **I, II, III**
SON OF A DOPE FIEND I II
HEAVEN GOT A GHETTO
Renta
GORILLAZ IN THE BAY **I II III IV**
TEARS OF A GANGSTA I II
3X KRAZY I II
DE'KARI
TRIGGADALE I II III
Elijah R. Freeman
GOD BLESS THE TRAPPERS I, II, III
THESE SCANDALOUS STREETS I, II, III
FEAR MY GANGSTA I, II, III IV, V
THESE STREETS DON'T LOVE NOBODY I, II
BURY ME A G I, II, III, IV, V
A GANGSTA'S EMPIRE I, II, III, IV
THE DOPEMAN'S BODYGAURD I II
THE REALEST KILLAZ I II III
THE LAST OF THE OGS
Tranay Adams
THE STREETS ARE CALLING
Duquie Wilson

MARRIED TO A BOSS... I II III

By Destiny Skai & Chris Green

KINGZ OF THE GAME I II III IV V

Playa Ray

SLAUGHTER GANG I II III

RUTHLESS HEART I II III

By Willie Slaughter

FUK SHYT

By Blakk Diamond

DON'T F#CK WITH MY HEART I II

By Linnea

ADDICTED TO THE DRAMA I II III

IN THE ARM OF HIS BOSS II

By Jamila

YAYO I II III IV

A SHOOTER'S AMBITION I II

By S. Allen

TRAP GOD I II III

By Troublesome

FOREVER GANGSTA

GLOCKS ON SATIN SHEETS I II

By Adrian Dulan

TOE TAGZ I II III

LEVELS TO THIS SHYT

By Ah'Million

KINGPIN DREAMS I II

C.R.E.A.M. 2

By Paper Boi Rari
CONFESSIONS OF A GANGSTA I II III
By Nicholas Lock
I'M NOTHING WITHOUT HIS LOVE
SINS OF A THUG
By Monet Dragun
CAUGHT UP IN THE LIFE I II III
By Robert Baptiste
NEW TO THE GAME I II III
MONEY, MURDER & MEMORIES I II
By **Malik D. Rice**
LIFE OF A SAVAGE I II III
A GANGSTA'S QUR'AN I II III
MURDA SEASON I II III
GANGLAND CARTEL I II III
CHI'RAQ GANGSTAS I II III
KILLERS ON ELM STREET
JACK BOYZ N DA BRONX
By **Romell Tukes**
LOYALTY AIN'T PROMISED I II
By Keith Williams
QUIET MONEY I II III
THUG LIFE I II III
EXTENDED CLIP I II
By **Trai'Quan**

Yolanda Moore

THE STREETS MADE ME I II
By **Larry D. Wright**
THE ULTIMATE SACRIFICE I, II, III, IV, V, VI
KHADIFI
IF YOU CROSS ME ONCE
ANGEL I II
By **Anthony Fields**
THE LIFE OF A HOOD STAR
By **Ca$h & Rashia Wilson**
THE STREETS WILL NEVER CLOSE
By **K'ajji**
CREAM I II
By **Yolanda Moore**
NIGHTMARES OF A HUSTLA I II
By **King Dream**
CONCRETE KILLAZ
By **Kingpen**
HARD AND RUTHLESS
By **Von Wiley Hall**
GHOST MOB II
Stilloan Robinson
MOB TIES
By **SayNoMore**
BODYMORE MURDERLAND
By **Delmont Player**
FOR THE LOVE OF A BOSS

C.R.E.A.M. 2

By C. D. Blue

<u>BOOKS BY LDP'S CEO, CA$H</u>

<u>TRUST IN NO MAN</u>

<u>TRUST IN NO MAN 2</u>

<u>TRUST IN NO MAN 3</u>

<u>BONDED BY BLOOD</u>

<u>SHORTY GOT A THUG</u>

<u>THUGS CRY</u>

<u>THUGS CRY 2</u>

<u>THUGS CRY 3</u>

<u>TRUST NO BITCH</u>

<u>TRUST NO BITCH 2</u>

<u>TRUST NO BITCH 3</u>

<u>TIL MY CASKET DROPS</u>

<u>RESTRAINING ORDER</u>

<u>RESTRAINING ORDER 2</u>

<u>IN LOVE WITH A CONVICT</u>

<u>LIFE OF A HOOD STAR</u>

C.R.E.A.M. 2